Text Classics

JULIAN RANDOLPH 'MICK' STOW was born in Geraldton, Western Australia, in 1935. He attended local schools before boarding at Guildford Grammar in Perth, where the renowned author Kenneth Mackenzie had been a student.

While at university he sent his poems to a British publisher. The resulting collection, *Act One*, won the Australian Literature Society's Gold Medal in 1957—as did the prolific young writer's third novel, *To the Islands*, the following year. *To the Islands* also won the 1958 Miles Franklin Literary Award. Stow reworked the novel for a second edition almost twenty-five years later, but never allowed its two predecessors to be republished.

He worked briefly as an anthropologist's assistant in New Guinea—an experience that subsequently informed *Visitants*, one of three masterful late novels—then fell seriously ill and returned to Australia. In the 1960s he lectured at universities in Australia and England, and lived in America on a Harkness fellowship. He published his second collection of verse, *Outrider*; the novel *Tourmaline*, on which critical opinion was divided; and his most popular fiction, *The Merry-Go-Round in the Sea* and *Midnite*.

For years afterwards Stow produced mainly poetry, libretti and reviews. In 1969 he settled permanently in England: first in Suffolk, then in Essex, where he moved in 1981. He received the 1979 Patrick White Award.

Randolph Stow died in 2010, aged seventy-four. A private man, a prodigiously gifted yet intermittently silent author, he has been hailed as 'the least visible figure of that great twentieth-century triumvirate of Australian novelists whose other members are Patrick White and Christina Stead'.

GABRIELLE CAREY is the author of novels, biography, autobiography, essays and, most recently, *Moving Among Strangers: Randolph Stow and My Family*, which was the joint winner of the 2014 Prime Minister's Literary Award for Non-Fiction. She teaches writing at the University of Technology Sydney.

ALSO BY RANDOLPH STOW

A Haunted Land
The Bystander
To the Islands
The Merry-Go-Round in the Sea
Midnite: The Story of a Wild Colonial Boy
Visitants
The Girl Green as Elderflower
The Suburbs of Hell

Tourmaline
Randolph Stow

Text Publishing Melbourne Australia

textclassics.com.au
textpublishing.com.au

The Text Publishing Company
Swann House
22 William Street
Melbourne Victoria 3000
Australia

First published by Macdonald, London, 1963
This edition published by The Text Publishing Company, 2015

Cover design by WH Chong
Page design by Text
Typeset by Midland Typesetters

Printed in Australia by Griffin Press, an Accredited ISO AS/NZS 14001:2004 Environmental Management System printer

Primary print ISBN: 9781925240306
Ebook ISBN: 9781922253118
Creator: Stow, Randolph, 1935–2010.
Title: Tourmaline / by Randolph Stow ; introduced by Gabrielle Carey.
Series: Text classics.
Dewey Number: A823.3

This book is printed on paper certified against the Forest Stewardship Council® Standards. Griffin Press holds FSC chain-of-custody certification SGS-COC-005088. FSC promotes environmentally responsible, socially beneficial and economically viable management of the world's forests.

CONTENTS

Fraught with Danger and Promise

by Gabrielle Carey

WHEN THE actor, director and writer Rachel Ward arrived in Australia from England, a friend handed her two books. If you want to understand this country, he said, these are your essential texts. One of them was *The Timeless Land*, by Eleanor Dark. The other was *Tourmaline*, by Randolph Stow.

There is something quintessentially Australian about *Tourmaline*. The outback town could be any outback town, the pub any rural pub at the end of 'the raw red streak of the road'. The landscape of dust and flies is instantly recognisable. But what is this book about a stranger who comes to a once-prosperous mining town now stricken by drought and promises to find water? Is it fable or allegory, a Western, or a philosophical examination of the differences between Christianity and Taoism?

Tourmaline was published in England in 1963 and subsequently greeted with bewilderment in Australia. Dame Leonie Kramer dismissed it as '*The Waste Land* with a few more bar scenes'. Anthony J. Hassall calls it Stow's least understood book. It is one of the most overtly modernist of his nine novels—at least of the early half dozen, published between 1956 and 1967—and the author's favourite, perhaps because it combined his talents as poet and prose writer. Indeed, the first few lines could easily be reformatted into poetry:

> I say we have a bitter heritage, but that is not to run it down. Tourmaline is the estate, and if I call it heritage I do not mean that we are free in it. More truly we are tenants; tenants of shanties rented from the wind, tenants of the sunstruck miles.

The pairing of poetry and prose is just one of many twin themes in *Tourmaline*, among them what Stow might have called the dual myths of Australia: paradise and prison, antipodean Eden and waterless wasteland, land of the spirit and of the Antichrist. The novel's narrator—Tourmaline's oldest resident, mysteriously named the Law—tells us that his town once had a crystalline lake and Babylonian hanging gardens. Now it is barren, dusty and sterile.

Like Australia, democratic and egalitarian, 'Tourmaline is a great leveller.' Of the men on the veranda of the pub, the Law tells us: 'Their clothes, their bark faces, their attitudes were identical.' Tourmaline is isolated from the rest of the world, the only contact a supply truck that arrives from 'the back of the blue ranges' each month. 'All of us, all Tourmaline, gathered in the street. And the truck slowly coming, its hot green paint powdered with Tourmaline dust, a grotesque hand of yellow metal dangling beside the driver's door. Waiting, all of us.'

Into this scene, with its echoes of Beckett's *Godot*, arrives a stranger. Off the back of the truck, like cargo, Michael Random is unloaded, scarred with a stigmata of sorts and terribly burned from the desert sun. The townsfolk gather round to revive him. When asked who he is, he answers: 'I'm—ah—diviner.' Stow's irony is so quiet it can sometimes go unnoticed. A water diviner who has almost died of thirst?

After the townsfolk save his life, he is expected to save theirs. Random is received as a messiah and the people place their faith in his supernatural ability to divine water. They trust in his promise to return Tourmaline to its mythical origins of lush greens and abundant water, a coloniser's nostalgic fantasy—the dream of England's verdant fields. Visions 'arose of a Tourmaline greater and richer even than in its heyday, a town paved with gold…inhabited solely by millionaires'.

Like the Biblical desert fathers, the diviner has come out of the desolate emptiness. Like Leichhardt, and Burke and Wills, he displays a 'gallant folly': perhaps another quintessentially Australian characteristic. But he has lost his divining rod, lost that which gives him direction and power.

As the diviner slowly recovers, his skin begins to peel. Again with gentle humour, Stow writes: 'On the third day he shaved,' a domestic and profoundly un-supernatural activity, playfully resonating with 'he rose again the third day.' And as the diviner rises from his convalescent bed, the town falls under his spell. All except Tom Spring, the storekeeper. Whereas the rest of the community is looking for a cure—for their lack of water, purpose, belief—Spring warns against the seductions of the diviner, remembering similar 'lunatics in the past': 'These black-and-white men… these poor holy hillbillies who can only think in terms of God and the devil.'

Random is the evangelist-preacher and Spring the quiet Taoist. When the Law asks Spring to outline his alternative faith, then says that the explanation is almost meaningless, Spring responds: 'Words can't cope…Your prophet knows how to cut the truth to fit the language. You don't get much truth, of course, but it's well-tailored.'

The residents of Tourmaline are looking for someone who can bring them together, enlighten them and, above all, save them. They believe that Random will make the desert bloom again. (Although his surname tells us that anyone might have played this role.) 'So wild was the optimism that there seemed to be a hazy feeling that the drought might break with the diviner's coming, and the millionaires go yachting on Lake Tourmaline.'

Even the Aboriginal people from the camp outside town, like Charlie Yandana, are swept up. They think that the diviner is the incarnation of Mongga, the water and fertility spirit. Tom Spring's 'half-caste' foster daughter, Deborah, also looks to the diviner, hoping that he might save her from her relationship with the brutish publican Kestrel. She sits in the bar 'wrapped in her clouds of exile', perhaps a little like Stow himself.

After the publication of *Tourmaline*, Stow decided to settle permanently in England, only returning to Australia twice. There were many reasons for his self-exile, but the uncomprehending reception of *Tourmaline* may well have contributed to his frustration with Australia, a frustration expressed by the young Rick in Stow's next and most popular novel, *The Merry-Go-Round in the Sea*.

Stow was so perplexed by the Australian response to the Taoist elements in *Tourmaline* that in the mid-1960s he published a series of poems entitled 'The Testament of Tourmaline: Variations on Themes of the *Tao Teh Ching*'. The original Lao Tzu text is:

> Tao wells up
> Like warm artesian waters.
>
> Multiple, unchanging,
> Like forms of water,
> It is cloud and pool,
> ocean and lake and river.

Stow's version reads:

> Deep. Go deep,
> as the long roots of myall
> mine the red country
> for water, for silence.
>
> Silence is water.
> All things are stirring,
> all things are flowering,
> rooted in silence.

The search for real water in a desert can only be a mirage. Stow suggests that the country needs not the divining of gold or water, but rather, as Hassall has observed, 'the divining of a true identity that will unite the land and its people'.

Metaphysics and mysticism aside, *Tourmaline* is a richly poetic novel with a visceral Australian atmosphere: 'the smell of sweat was overlaid with the clean and bitter tang of dust. Perhaps a sharper scent was there, too, from the leaves of myall baking in the sun.' So lyrical is the prose that an opera of *Tourmaline* was drafted in the early 1970s, with a libretto by Richard Fotheringham and music by Robert Keane. The performer and composer Iain Grandage has set extracts of *Tourmaline* to music, and the theatre director Andrew Ross has staged adaptations. Rachel Ward is writing the screenplay for a film version.

Tourmaline is more relevant now than ever. A note at the beginning instructs the reader that 'The action of the novel is to be imagined as taking place in the future.' Stow's apocalyptic vision of a formerly wealthy mining city is prophetic. As I write this, there are reports that Broken Hill may run out of water. Its mayor is assuring residents of the treatability of bore water. Ours is a country immeasurably rich in resources, yet our most precious resource is also our most scarce.

In one scene of the novel the townsfolk congregate at the war memorial at the call of the bugle. It seems like an ordinary Anzac Day ceremony, the kind that most Australians have attended. But the Law tells the assembled people that there is a curse on them all—for the unexplained 'terrible things' that happened there in the past.

This is partly why the townspeople fall for the cult of the diviner. They hope for the town to be reborn; the Law looks forward to a change in the weather and plans an Edenic garden free of sin. Yet, in the world of *Tourmaline*, there 'is no sin but cruelty. Only one. And that original sin, that began when a man first cried to another, in his matted hair: Take charge of my life, I am close to breaking.' Stow suggests that cults prey on two common human frailties: the desire for someone else to 'take charge' of our lives, and self-loathing. (Tom Spring argues with the Law: 'And how is it, anyway, that you've lived all these years and not seen that a man who hates himself is the only kind of wild beast we have to watch for?') Michael Random offers to relieve the townspeople of the burden of responsibility, of living for themselves.

Spring's final words, and perhaps the key to the philosophy behind all of Stow's fiction, are: 'Honour the single soul.' With this new edition of *Tourmaline*, we honour the singular soul of Randolph Stow.

Tourmaline

Ô gens de peu de poids
dans la mémoire de ces
lieux...

St-John Perse: ANABASE

NOTE

The action of this novel is to be imagined
as taking place in the future.

A first draft of Chapter 1 was published
in *Meanjin*, No. 85 (1961).

For M.C.S.

ONE

I say we have a bitter heritage, but that is not to run it down. Tourmaline is the estate, and if I call it heritage I do not mean that we are free in it. More truly we are tenants; tenants of shanties rented from the wind, tenants of the sunstruck miles. Nevertheless I do not scorn Tourmaline. Even here there is something to be learned; even groping through the red wind, after the blinds of dust have clattered down, we discover the taste of perfunctory acts of brotherhood: warm, acidic, undemanding, fitting a derelict independence. Furthermore, I am not young.

There is no stretch of land on earth more ancient than this. And so it is blunt and red and barren, littered with the fragments of broken mountains, flat, waterless. Spinifex grows here, but sere and yellow, and trees are rare, hardly to be called trees, some kind of myall with leaves starved to needles that fans out from the root and gives no shade.

At times, in the early morning, you would call this a gentle country. The new light softens it, tones flow a little, away from the stark forms. It is at dawn that the sons of Tourmaline feel for their heritage. Grey of dead wood, grey-green of leaves, set off a soil bright and tender, the tint of blood in water. Those are the colours of Tourmaline. There is a fourth, to the far west, the deep blue of hills barely climbing the horizon. But that is the colour of distance, and no part of Tourmaline, belonging more to the sky.

It is not the same country at five in the afternoon. That is the hardest time, when all the heat of the day rises, and every pebble glares, wounding the eyes, shortening the breath; the time when the practice of living is hardest to defend, and nothing seems easier than to cease, to become a stone, hot and still. At five in the afternoon there is one colour only, and that is brick-red, burning. After sunset, the blue dusk, and later the stars. The sky is the garden of Tourmaline.

To describe the town, I must begin with the sun. The sun is close here. If you look at Tourmaline, shade your eyes. It is a town of corrugated iron, and in the heat the corrugations shimmer and twine, strangely immaterial. This is hard to watch, and the glare of the stony ground is cruel.

The road ends here. There is a broken fence to show it, its posts leaning, its barbed wire trailing to the ground. Facing this, the Tourmaline war memorial, a modest obelisk, convenient for dogs and the weary. Some sons of Tourmaline, it seems, patronized the empire in the days of the Boer War, but not much is remembered. To the right is Tom Spring's store, the white paint flaking from its iron and the purple paint from its ancient advertisement for

Bushell's tea. In the window, shaded by a rough veranda, tinned food, soap, cutlery and boots cradle the immemorial cat of T. & M. Spring.

On the left is Kestrel's Tourmaline Hotel, of stone and rough plaster, once whitewashed, but now reddened with dust. The roofing iron is also red, and advertises a brand of beer no longer brewed. A veranda shades the bare dirt on three sides. In this hot metallic shade Kestrel's dog wakes and yawns, and sleeps again. The windows are closed, and painted inside. It is dim in there.

Following the raw red streak of the road are the houses of Tourmaline: uniform, dilapidated, stained with the red dust. There are not many. At last, and apart, is a cube of stone, marked by a wooden sign as the police station. And behind it rises a fortress, a squat square tower open to the sky. This is my tower and prison; for I am the Law of Tourmaline.

On two stony hills to the north of the town stand the toppling masts of the mine and the hulk of the abandoned church. The church is of tender brown and rose stone. Beside it, an oleander impossibly persists in flowering. Planks are falling from the wooden bell tower, but the bell is there still; and in dust-storms and on nights of high wind its irregular tolling sweeps away over Tourmaline to the south.

From there you command the whole town: the rust-red roofs, the skeletal obelisks of headless windmills, the sudden green of Rock's forlorn garden. That is all there is of Tourmaline.

A man called Hart found gold here, many years ago. Others came. The gold was sufficient, it seems, and there

7

was water in those days. I can remember the water. I can remember rain in Tourmaline. I am not young.

It is not a ghost town. It simply lies in a coma. This may never end.

On the day he came, the diviner, we had a death in Tourmaline. But it was not one of importance. Billy Bogada, in the native camp, was noticed by his nephews, when they rolled out at daybreak, to have departed. The women mourned a little, out of courtesy, and the nephews went to Tom Spring for a packing-case the size of the deceased. I watched them, later in the day, carry him down the road to the cemetery; their skins shining in the glare of the stony ground, the box on their faded blue cotton shoulders. SPRING—it said. PERISHABLE.

Charlie Yandana sang, squatting on the ground outside my door, in the narrow shade of the dead pepper tree. He was young, and not bereaved, but he liked to sing. It was a hymn, perhaps.

> Death, oh death, oh
> you been going a long time now.
> When you gunna take a rest,
> oh death?

His voice, young and flippant, made me desolate. I had had my morning rendezvous with the world, my walk to the war memorial, and so come to the time of day when I doubt the reality of myself. Those names give me a name. But when I am quiet and alone, and have turned on the wireless (as on every morning for—ah, too many years) and

8

have spoken, and have listened, and as on every morning since these terrible times began have heard no answer—when I am quiet and alone I cannot believe in it. Who gave me this name? And beside the name, what is there? An unnamed and naming ghost, perhaps, formless, but forming for some obscure purpose of its own a room of pale stone, ledges heaped with red dust, a shelf of tattered books, a cupboard, a safe. Then detail derides the egoism. What use has this mind for the rusty handcuffs hung on the doorframe, the map of Western Australia, the legs of Charlie Yandana sweating in the sun? The house I haunt is furnished and inhabited. A terrible loneliness is touched by the young voice.

So I resented Charlie Yandana. But I did not speak to him. Silence is a habit as enslaving as the most delicate vice, and as time goes on to talk (to talk, that is, to anything but the waiting, perhaps, but forever unanswering wireless) becomes embarrassing, as if, shaving, one should address some remark to the mirror and be overheard. I find that there is no speech that is not soliloquy. And yet, always, I sense an audience.

When the singing stopped, the silence reached around us. Morning and noon passed with variations of shadow, slight mutations of light. The blotches on my hands made me think of age. What enormous and desolate landscapes are opened by the voice of a lone crow.

There is much I must invent, much I have not seen. Guesses, hints, like pockets of dust in the crevices of conversation. And Tourmaline will not believe me.

But (dear God) what is Tourmaline, and where? I am alone. I write my testament for myself to read. I will prove to myself there has been life on this planet.

The cells are unroofed, the bars are gone. Records of intriguing crimes and acts of justice blow in the yard. In other places, it is believed that Tourmaline is dead.

There is no law in Tourmaline: this is known there. The gaol abandoned and crumbling, the gaoler dead. So all must assume.

Yet I live on, prisoner of my ruined tower; my keys turned on myself now all the locks are gone.

The Law of Tourmaline. Guessing, inventing. Ghost of a house furnished and inhabited, tormented by the persistence of the living.

On the long bar of Kestrel's hotel (that day and every day, you must imagine) were three fly-traps. And the prisoners climbed and fell back continually with a soft, intermittent, sickening fizz. Glasses and elbows and stains of liquor surrounded them. The window-panes were painted over, the air was close, but cooler; the smell of sweat was overlaid with the clean and bitter tang of dust. Perhaps a sharper scent was there, too, from the leaves of myall baking in the sun.

A road of daylight led from the open door to the cash-register, striking deep jewel-tones from liqueurs that will never be drunk in Tourmaline. It struck, also, a gold bangle on the wrist of Deborah, in which the sombre green of the walls merged with the tawny glimmer of her half-caste skin.

It rose on Deborah herself, very tall, very straight; her back uncompromising and austere, her calm hands folded.

That tallness had entered into her character, making her remote; almost, at times (that aloofness partly obscuring her), invisible. But she was timid, too; the profound darkness of her eyes unwilling to be looked into. Imagine her there.

Unlistening, wrapped in her clouds of exile; absorbed in her bangle, in which the room had intruded a confused and gentler impression of itself.

While Kestrel, a thin black line in the bangle, leaned over the bar and talked to Rock; the black forelock overhanging his black Celt's brow, and his face suggesting experience of every bitterness the world had to offer. And yet he was not old (at thirty-five, alas), not ugly, not acquainted with life beyond Tourmaline. The bitterness lay not in the lines of his face (which was smooth, almost a mask) but in the thin, bent, vulnerable lips; and there was a little, more than a little, in the soft voice. And yet, at least until Deborah came to distract him from drink, there was something altogether conflicting to be surprised at times in his eyes. Imagine him there.

And (Rock speaking) looking round, perhaps, at her. And she then, aware of him, of course, in her bangle, lifting her head to meet his eyes. But never smiling, neither one. It was always and only that: the encounter of eyes staring as through windows, and the whole room filled with despair.

A strange love indeed. Yet they loved—bitterly.

Once he said, interrupting Rock: 'What are you dreaming about?'

And Deborah, her eyes down on her bangle again, murmured: 'When will the truck come?'

11

And so, a communication made. Incapable of conversation, both of them, except with others. But all day and night they would be throwing words at one another, words meaning all one thing. Look, I am here, I have not gone from you, not yet.

And imagine Rock, made sad by them, gazing into his rum. A martyr to sadness, that large and wooden man. Draining his glass and picking up his hat, and turning towards Deborah to nod to her, or smile, or something; but finding her drowned in her bangle. And so going past her, and into the street of Tourmaline—that road I have described already, as soft with dust underfoot as if carpeted with red fur, but hot and solid rock below for all that.

And they behind him, in their desperate room, saying nothing. The air dull and heavy, the light greenish. A clock cutting across the sizzling of the captive flies.

Easy, easy to imagine them there forever; and the red dust rising to bury them as they stand, like the householders of Pompeii.

To begin, I must imagine and invent.

Tom Spring, on a rickety chair, behind the counter of his store, sleeves rolled up on his thin strong arms. A small strong thin man, Tom; quiet, so quiet one might stop and listen, in surprise. A deep Quaker quiet, an act of religion, that might help his soul to become like a great cave and trap and amplify the faint whisperings of God—that was the silence he was building, behind his quiet eyes, under his thinning hair. Imagine him there.

A fly or two whining and bumping at the window.

And the cat rapt, oblivious, like one who has received enlightenment.

And Mary, in the kitchen perhaps, or coming in to spray the flies (which, it could be, she heard from another room, shattering the holy calm), with her dark greying hair and her plump arms, her immovable charity. Imagine her there.

And the belts, boots, billy cans, bridles and halters and flypapers hanging from the rafters. The rust. The dust—needing no apology, since Tourmaline dust is nothing if not sterile. The piles of blankets and shirts, of trousers and tinned food, on tables and shelves.

And the flies, on their backs, kicking and fizzing a little before dying. And then silence, unbroken even by God.

Outside, under Kestrel's veranda, men sat in the dust; propped against a wall, sharp knees drawn up, with glasses in their hands. Ah, Tourmaline is a great leveller. Their clothes, their bark faces, their attitudes were identical; their lassitude was a communal affair, or perhaps a form of pestilence. And under Tom Spring's veranda two tired black men lay asleep.

And Byrne was there, sprawled across the step of the war memorial with his guitar; drunk, his eyes in their cavernous sockets obscure with it, satanic eyebrows bent like a pair of kylies. Kestrel's cousin, poor Byrnie, with his devilish face and no vice in him. A gentle man, and virtuous too (but indeed there is not much scope for sin in Tourmaline). Imagine him there.

Calling out to Rock, perhaps: 'I'm broke, Rocky. Ah Rocky, I'm not drunk enough.'

Or singing, brushing the sharp chords from his guitar.

Then, in the distance, a cloud of dust, a glint of metal. A murmur rising among the lounging bodies. 'The truck. The truck.' And Kestrel issuing from his door, and Mary Spring from hers.

And I myself appearing, pacing the road from my prison with long authoritative strides. My hair grey and streaked like last year's stubble, my face like an aerial photograph of the most barren ranges in the land. Imagine me well.

All of us, all Tourmaline, gathered in the street. And the truck slowly coming, its hot green paint powdered with Tourmaline dust, a grotesque hand of yellow metal dangling beside the driver's door. Waiting, all of us.

All but Byrne; who swept the chords of his guitar, and sang a song of his Scottish forebears, keening in drunken grief.

'New Holland is a barren place,
in it there grows no grain,
nor any habitation
wherein for to remain...'

TWO

Perhaps it was natural that we should be in awe of him, the driver of the truck. After all, it was many years that he had been coming, once a month, from the back of the blue ranges; and always he hugged to himself the mystery of his life's true ambience, as if it could endanger us. He would hardly speak. He was as zealous as a grandmother guarding the facts of life. There were days when he might take a glass of rum from Kestrel, exchange a few words with him about certain dealings in gold (which, when I was young, would have been illicit, though who cares now?); but then, warily, huskily taking his leave, he would climb again into the sweating cab of his truck beside the obelisk, which the bystanders in the meantime would have unloaded, and without a wave creep away, through the galah-feather dust, towards his home behind the hills. And for days, some-times, his tyre-marks would remain with us, to remind us of his reality; but as soon as the first wind erased them he became insubstantial, and our memories could not re-create him, could seize on nothing but the dangling yellow hand beside his door.

So, on this day, he came, and stealthily swept around the obelisk to pull up by Kestrel's veranda. And Kestrel and I, the town's senior citizens, came forward, to do him the greater honour.

He climbed out slowly, even majestically: there was something majestic in his solitude. He advanced a step or two to meet us. A small man, really, in dirty khaki, with great reaching eyebrows like the antennae of moths, and a thin insect-voice, drowsy, like locusts, as I remember them long ago in fallow fields when I was young.

I listened to his insect-voice. I did not hear his words. He lulled me, with the recollection of summer paddocks. He was saying: 'I want some help,' and it seemed mysterious, unlikely. I looked at Kestrel, who was watching the small man.

'I've got a bloke here,' the driver said. So calmly, it seemed impossible. 'I picked a bloke up on the road.'

Byrne was on the other side of the truck, his guitar in his dusty hand. 'You picked a bloke up?' he called across. 'Where in God's name did you find a bloke?'

'He was lying on the road,' the driver said. 'He's bad. I think he's finished.' And so coldly he said it, in his insect-voice, that I felt once again the danger—the terrible danger—ah, I cannot tell what terrible danger I appre-hended from behind those blue hills.

But Tourmaline was agog. Rock and Mary were

16

standing beside us, and their eyes were avid. Jack Speed, who was holding up Byrne (he swayed somewhat), looked like a child at Christmas. Horse Carson called: 'Where is he?' with all the eagerness of a fasting cannibal. One could read it in every face: an event had occurred, an event whose magnitude and significance Tourmaline had difficulty in estimating.

The driver waved at the truck; and slowly, majestically, walked round to the other door. Kestrel and I followed at his heels, and the rest massed about us. Strangely (I cannot express it) it seemed like an unveiling; such a ceremony as I think the dedication of our noble obelisk never was, far, far more mysterious, fraught with danger and promise. And I felt, as the small man reached up his arm to the handle of the high door and I noticed the golden glint of the fuzz on his arm, I felt, deep inside me—such curious yearnings.

Kestrel was beside me as the door opened. For a second I glimpsed the figure inside it, a man also in stained khaki, who had been slumped against the door. For a second only. And then he began to fall.

But Kestrel reached up and caught him. And that was how we first saw the diviner; his yellow hair, streaked and sun-bleached, on Kestrel's shoulder, and one blistered and swollen arm hanging limp down Kestrel's back.

Weaker and more helpless than the smallest child in Kestrel's arms. And when I think back I wonder if we didn't, in those first days, see the truth of him. But no, there was more, there must have been. It was only Kestrel who was deceived by that complete surrender. He was more,

17

far more; but not at that moment. Then, he was helpless, defeated. And disfigured—terribly. But he had been far, so far, in country never mapped, on the border-lands of death. He had been where Kestrel had not, where none of us had ever been. And he brought news.

But not at that moment. Then, he was limper than an infant; and the sight of his dreadful arm against Kestrel's shirt was too much, too much for me.

'Ah, Christ,' Kestrel said. He had moved back a little, very gently. 'Ah, Jesus Christ, the poor bastard.'

And Mary Spring, when she had seen the stranger's face, did not object to this rude compassion.

I came to Kestrel's side and took the sagging body by the waist. We laid him down in the dust, in the truck's narrow shadow. He had a golden beard, of about a fortnight's growth. And his hair was like hay, like the outside of a new stack, after the first few rains.

But his face was terrible and enormous, swollen to huge size and burning like the sun. He had no eyes, it seemed. The lids had swelled till they appeared to fill the sockets, he could not have opened them. And above all that was his bright young hair.

'He'll die,' Byrne said. 'Will he die, Kes?' No one had ever heard him so hushed.

'Oh, he's young,' Mary Spring said; praying, I suspect. 'Deborah, look, he's quite young.'

'How could you tell?' Rock asked her. 'He hasn't got a face, properly speaking.'

'His hair,' Deborah said. 'His hair's young, Rocky.'

'About my age,' said Jack Speed, who was twenty-five.

18

'And not likely to get much older,' said Horse Carson.

'Kes, is he going to die?'

Kestrel was impatient. 'How should I know?' He mused over the ruined face, enquiring: 'Is he conscious?'

'He was,' the driver said. 'Just. I picked him up by the side of the road, fifty miles back. Had to manhandle him into the truck.'

He stood aloof, meanwhile, one hand on the truck door. The droning voice floated down to me from the sky as I kneeled by the prone man. I listened to the painful breath force its way through the huge lips, thinking—what was I thinking?—a life, a new life in Tourmaline, a life to save, a life. So precious it seemed, of such incalculable value. A life for Tourmaline.

Kestrel, beside me, looked up at the standing man. He asked: 'Do you want to take him back with you?'

'What for?' The driver sounded as if he genuinely wished to know. 'He's had it, that's for sure.' And I thought again of the terrible danger, feeling angry and afraid.

'He'll stay here, then,' Kestrel said; slowly, even doubt-fully, because this was after all an unheard-of experiment. 'All right. I'll have him.'

'No,' Mary said. She was quite determined.

Kestrel got up off his haunches and looked at her, grinning a little with his bitter mouth. 'Why's that, Mary?'

'We'll have him,' she said.

'You think I ought to trade you this bloke for Deborah?'

'Kes,' Deborah said, hating him.

'All right, all right,' Kestrel said, 'you can have him. Let's get him inside, that's all.' He bent down and lifted the

19

man's limp body, with his hands under the stiff dry cloth at the armpits.

In the meantime, since Horse and Rock and two natives had unloaded the truck of its cargo of such food and liquor and kerosene as Tourmaline can afford, the driver had gone round to the other door. We were startled by the sudden slam of it. He was sitting there, high up, behind the steering wheel.

'You going?' Byrne called out.

The driver answered him by starting the engine.

'You bastard,' Byrne suddenly yelled at him. 'You slimy black bastard. I hope you break down and fry in your syphilitic bloody truck.'

But the truck was already moving, the driver heard nothing. Slowly he slid away, towards the red road and the ranges, remote, mysterious. And Byrne, meanwhile, clutching his guitar in the middle of the road, was weeping with rage and pity. This was the eccentricity of Byrne, that drink brought him to tears.

And the diviner lay now in the open sun, looking very terrible. It was too much, too much to bear. We wanted to cover him, even bury him, anything rather than to go on looking at the monstrous joke of his face.

'Jack. Horse,' Kestrel said. 'Lend a hand to carry him into Tom's.' But he himself retired to the shade of his own doorway, and stood there bleakly watching.

So three men lifted the diviner, and carried him across the wide street into Tom Spring's house of silence; where Tom, looking up, vaguely, from some book he was reading, said: 'Ah. Has the truck come, already?'

*

I should explain that relations between Kestrel and Mary Spring were on the strained side; and the cause was not her piety or his lack of it, but Deborah. For Deborah had lived in the Springs' house since her sixth year, when her mother (who had been given the name of Agnes Day, as a compliment to Jesus) broke a bottle of rum, half a dozen eggs and her neck by falling down an abandoned shaft near the native camp. She was drunk, of course, and Mary blamed the calamity on the young Kestrel, who took no notice. There were some who suggested that Deborah was the daughter of Mary's late uncle; but as there were few men in Tourmaline who might not have fathered a child on Agnes Day, no judgement was ever taken. Whatever the reason, Mary fostered Deborah, and loved her, and brought her up to be as promising a girl as had been seen in Tourmaline since Mary herself was young. And one day, six months before this event, Deborah had walked across the road to the hotel, and stayed there.

Her 'marriage' (I must use the terms of Tourmaline) remained as mysterious as her paternity. But still Mary hoped, and plotted to win the girl away from Kestrel, whose imposing double bed had had more and darker occupants than Deborah (indeed, Agnes Day was one of them), though never for so long. What husband Mary had in mind for her daughter we did not discover; Jack Speed, perhaps, or even middle-aged Rocky—who could say? It was enough for Kestrel that she detested him. That was why he watched so dourly as Deborah followed the cortege through Tom Spring's door.

When Tom saw the body, he gave a sudden quick: 'Ah,' and came around the counter to us. He was a long time studying the face of our burden, and we waited meanwhile in silence; in expectation, too, I think, as if Tom might be able to decipher this extraordinary augury, which for all of us remained so inscrutable. But he said nothing in the end, only moved aside for Mary to open the door into the living quarters of the store, through which we bore him to a small room of white-washed iron, with a narrow iron bed, a cane chair, and a table supporting a basin and ewer which glared with roses.

We laid our charge on a sea-grass mat while Deborah fetched sheets and made the bed. Then, very gently, we stripped him of boots and socks, and slit up the sleeves and back of his shirt to avoid touching his forearms with the cloth. Over his left breast there was a hollow scar, and another on his back, opposite. We lifted him on to the bed and supported his head with pillows, and then Mary came with cloths and a bowl of reddish Tourmaline water, and damped the cloths and draped them on his forehead. I bear witness that in all things she behaved according to the directions of *Everything A Lady Should Know*, the property of Tom's grandmother.

But Rock said that was not enough, and taking the bowl from Mary he swabbed the man's body, and pulled the sheet over him and soaked that too. And then he said we must pull the bed out from the wall, and stand about and fan him, as that would be easier work than hewing a grave up on the hill there. He spoke as if only he appreciated the tremendous urgency of saving our patient for Tourmaline: but I think all of us felt this urgency, and a certain irritation with the others.

So we stood by the bedside. A strange sight we must have been, fanning with bits of paper and cardboard and whatever else came to hand, earnest, and almost silent. The two women were there, and Rock and I, and Byrne, who seemed quite sober now and very grave. Jack Speed and Horse Carson came and went throughout the afternoon. Horse dipped into our subject's trouser pockets for a name or some other clue, but there was nothing of that sort; only a pocket-knife, a handkerchief, a box of matches and a number of coins. 'He wasn't broke,' said Horse; adding: 'He's wet his pants, poor bugger.'

I remember the quiet of that afternoon, the forlorn crowing of Mary's one rooster in the yard outside, the hiss of wind through stiff leaves, the occasional useless clank of the Springs' windmill probing the almost dry bore. And above all the breathing of the man on the bed, who held on, who held so stubbornly on, defying the sun itself.

At times Mary took his temperature. We declared at first that the old thermometer lied, when it said a hundred and seven; but Rock, who seemed to know something about these things, said he trusted it. In all the afternoon there was little change; a degree or two at the most. Our wrists ached with fanning, our legs with standing. After sunset, Mary said there was no point in retaining so many nurses. She and Tom would care for their new protégé, she seemed to suggest; and the rest of us, I think, rather resented this hint of possessiveness. He belonged to Tourmaline, after all.

'I'll stay too,' Deborah said. And Mary nodded, looking pleased.

Byrne said, rather awkwardly: 'I'll keep night watch.'

'You, Byrnie,' Mary said. 'You'll be dead drunk by ten o'clock.'

He actually flushed, and muttered: 'Not tonight.'

'We'll get chairs, Deborah,' Mary said. So we knew then that we were dismissed.

We went out into the street, where Rock soon left us. The sky was of that turquoise, verging on green, that comes between sunset and darkness, and had one star in it. The land was lumpy and obscure. Byrne had picked up his guitar from Tom's counter. He sat down on the war memorial, strumming a little, moodily.

I stood near him, looking down, observing the thick black hair, the gaunt hollow of his cheek as he bent over the guitar, the one satanic eyebrow that was in my line of vision. In that faint light he looked melancholy and even distinguished. One could not see the ruined skin. Some adolescent complaint had robbed him of whatever beauty he might have had, leaving his face pitted with craters, like a dead dark moon.

He struck me as being intolerably sad. I said to him: 'I think this boy will live, Byrnie. Rocky thinks so, and he seems to know.'

He thumbed a chord or two, and said: 'Good old Rocky,' absently.

'Tourmaline seems to have taken charge of him. When he wakes up he's going to feel he's not his own property any more.'

'He mightn't want to be his own property,' Byrne said. 'Why would he?'

I was surprised, and said: 'Only a weak-willed man——'

'Ah, hell,' he suddenly shouted, striking loud discords. 'All right, I was meant to be someone's dog.' And he went

24

on to play some ballad, very loud and twanging, with his face turned away. I had hurt him, somehow.

So I said: 'Good night, Byrnie,' and left him, and went up the road towards my gaol. Towards my tower, silhouetted dark and square against the green western sky, and the black arms of my stricken tree, and the single soft wattle-ball of the evening star, which does not, alas, belong to me.

But his voice followed me far, lamenting.

'New Holland is a barren place,
in it there grows no grain,
nor any habitation
wherein for to remain...'

I pushed open my gate. I paused in my barren garden, beside the dead pepper tree.

'But the sugar-canes are plenty,
and the wine drops from the tree...'

I lit the hurricane lantern on the bench by the door, and entered my dark habitation.

Byrne, like most of Tourmaline, did a bit of fossicking to keep himself in liquor. But since he was lazy and unlucky, he also relied very often on the charity of his cousin Kestrel, for whom he did odd jobs round the hotel. Depending on his activities and his state of sobriety he had two homes: one a single-roomed miner's hut of dry stone on the hill behind the church, the other a small back room of the hotel containing only a bed, on which he had many times been dumped, like a bag of wheat, by sympathetic but

25

exasperated drinking-mates. On one celebrated occasion Kestrel and Horse Carson had succeeded in landing him on it by throwing him through the air from the doorway. He claimed to remember nothing of this, and to disbelieve it.

After I left him he did not start drinking again, but went to this room and lay down on the bed and messed about with his guitar. He was very thoughtful. Presently Kestrel stuck his head through the door, and said: 'Where's that bloody Deborah?' Byrne said that she was nursing the new bloke. 'Go and get her,' Kestrel said. 'I want to eat tonight.' But Byrne got up from the bed and said he would hash up a bit of tucker. He was very obliging.

In the course of the meal, which Kestrel ate between trips to the bar, Kestrel said that the bloke was sure to die and that Deborah might as well come home. Byrne said nothing. His cousin added that Byrne ate like an old dog, and that there was no necessity for it, as at least one part of his body, his teeth, was in fair condition. He considered, moreover, that if Byrne ate more and drank less he would be healthier and less of a drain on the pub's resources. Byrne concentrated on eating less obtrusively, and seemed to contemplate Kestrel's advice; which was odd, as it was not the first time he had heard it. He then stated that he was ready to shoot himself at any time, if Kestrel thought that was the best thing for him. Kestrel said: 'You corny bastard,' and went back to the bar.

Byrne washed up, taking care to keep as pure as possible the red water in the basin, which had still several days service to do. Then he returned to his bed, and went to sleep, eventually, still holding his guitar.

At eleven he woke again, and found Kestrel standing in the room with a lamp in his hand, looking blacker and more bitter than ever. Kestrel said: 'Deborah's still over there.'

'Watching the bloke,' Byrne said, squinting at the light.

'Go and get her for me, will you?'

Byrne rolled over, yawning. 'She wouldn't listen to me.'

'I'm not going,' Kestrel said. 'Not to start an argument with old Mary. Do me a favour.'

Byrne sat up and rubbed his eyes. When he thought about it, he seemed to like the idea. 'All right,' he said. 'I'll take over from her.' He pulled on his boots (Deborah was trying to domesticate him) and followed Kestrel through the hotel to the front door; through which the road showed all pale and silver-rose in the moonlight, and the Springs' white store gleamed like a tomb. There was no light there, but the sick man's room faced the yard in any case.

He crossed the road, his footprints making great pits of shadow in the soft dust, and walked round to the back of the store. A pale-yellow glow came from the sick-room, where Deborah sat in a cane chair by the bed, the lamp beside her, reading some aged magazine. I suppose it was the property of Tom's grandmother. He called to her from the window, and she rose and came to him.

'Kes wants you,' he said.

'Why?' she whispered back. And knowing him, I imagine that he blushed.

'I'll watch the bloke,' he said.

'You'll go to sleep.'

'I've slept already,' he told her. 'I'm sober, Deb. Honest.' He was very grave.

I can see her standing there, tall and slender in her blue dress, and glimmering a little, golden, in the lamplight. She loved Kestrel, and probably feared him too; but she also loved Mary, and had made her a promise. So she stood hesitating.

But Byrne already had one long thin blue denim leg over the window-sill, and had solved her problem to his own satisfaction. 'I'm sober,' he swore again. 'Go home, Deb. You haven't slept yet. Kes is waiting up for you.' And as she still hesitated, he picked her up, rather timorously, and lifted her through the window. There she stood, in the moonlight, thrust out; and the two blue moons reflected in her deep eyes gave her a slightly wild and captive look.

'Oh, all right,' she said at last. 'I suppose I have to. You won't sleep, Byrnie?'

'I won't sleep,' he promised. Then he turned away to look at the man on the bed, and forgot about her; so she paused no longer, but went out in the moonlight across the road, and through the lighted doorway of the hotel, where Kestrel seized her and enveloped her, like an octopus.

Byrne hung over the man on the bed, whose face and neck and arms had been anointed by Mary with a mixture of baking soda and Vaseline, till he resembled a dancer painted for corroboree. He put his hand on the bedaubed forehead. It was cooler, not so dry as it had been in the afternoon, and the breathing was now less painful. He dampened the cloths around the man's head, and neck, and sprinkled the sheet again, and sat down with the magazine to fan him and to watch. And he did watch, it seems, all night, he couldn't take his eyes from the patient; who

28

lay all this time exactly as we had placed him on the bed seven hours before, and stubbornly breathed on through his blubber-lips, oblivious.

Towards sunrise, when Byrne had blown the lamp out, and the walls and the sheets and the white blotches on the man's face were washed blue with the pre-dawn light, he began to stir and moan. Byrne leaned over him, and saw that he seemed to be trying to raise the swollen lids of his eyes (they too were plastered with Mary's preparation), and was even showing a little of the iris, of indistinguishable colour. Byrne rested his hand on the sufferer's hot chest, and placed his mouth close against him. 'Who are you?' he whispered.

The man moved his head, restlessly, and groaned. Suddenly he whispered, in a weak childish voice, what sounded like: 'Up to you.'

'What's your name?' Byrne asked. 'Your name, mate. Your name.'

After that the man on the bed was silent for a long time, and Byrne drew back. But then he began again, moving his head on the pillow, and moaning, and the feeble voice began to break into words, groups of words separated by gasping silences. 'Up to you,' he said. And then: 'To you, now… Don't want…can't take…not me to decide.' And later, after a long pause: 'Ah, piker! Oh God!' When that was said, his eyes closed again.

Byrne filled a glass from a jug of water on the table, lifted the man a little from the pillows and held it to his lips. For about a minute they sat there. Then the patient began to drink, sobbing and slobbering in his eagerness, and swallowed a second glassful after that, of our vile

Tourmaline water, before Byrne laid him down. He lay still then, panting.

'You're no piker, son,' Byrne said to him. 'What's your name?'

But the man on the bed did not speak again, and seemed to have fallen into a profound sleep. So Byrne desisted. He sat back in his chair and watched the dawn outside revive the delicate colour of red earth and grey-green leaves and grey myall-stems. The lone rooster flapped and crowed. The black cat leaped on to the window-sill and sat there, staring. At six o'clock Mary came in in her nightgown and said: 'Byrnie!' He grinned at her, diffident. Mary told me she had never seen him so pleased with himself.

It was about half-past ten when I came again, to inquire after the patient. Mary had been in the kitchen, and followed me into the little room where he lay, guarded once more by Deborah from her rickety chair. He had been anointed a second time with Mary's concoction, more thickly, and now looked less like a dancer than a clown. I asked whether he had been conscious.

'He spoke to Byrnie,' Mary said. 'Or raved. But he hasn't been conscious, no.'

'He's much better, though,' Deborah said. 'His skin's damp.' And she touched his pathetic white-washed forehead, very lightly, as if touching him meant something, and looked at us.

I suppose no one had spoken in that room for an hour or two: that may explain it. At any rate, we were suddenly startled by a very tired, but otherwise normal and even

30

pleasant male voice, which said, from behind Deborah's leaning body: 'Am I blind?'

Deborah moved back. There he lay, just as before. But he had spoken, evidently.

It was slightly uncanny. At length, as neither woman had answered, I moved to the foot of the bed, and looked up the length of him to his poor tragi-comic face, and asked: 'Are you awake?'

'Awake,' he said, his speech slurred a little by his great cumbersome lips, and sounding very weary and hesitant. But he went on, moving his head uneasily. 'Can't see, though. Eyes shut.'

'You've been badly burnt,' I told him. 'Your eyelids have swelled. But I think you can open them, if you try.' I hated the cold commonsense of my voice, even while I was speaking.

He took me at my word, however, screwing up his pale mask with the effort, and giving himself a certain amount of pain, it appeared. And he did succeed. Suddenly the heavy lids were halfway open, and he was looking towards me.

A strange effect, almost miraculous, to see a mask come alive; an event like birth or metamorphosis, very solemn, and slightly flavoured with the taste of tears. There he was: a life for Tourmaline, a life that we had saved. He was ours. And his eyes were very vivid, very blue, like the sudden kingfisher-flash down by the creek, at the end of the garden, at home, when I was young.

I asked: 'Can you see me?' An old man going soft at the heart had best keep to the bare necessities of speech. 'You're not blind, are you?'

31

'No,' he said, after staring at me for a time. He turned his head a little and studied Mary and Deborah. Then he lowered his gaze again.

'Does your head ache?' Deborah asked him.

'Yes,' he said, moving, restlessly. 'Doesn't matter. Doesn't matter. I don't——' But he seemed to forget whatever it was he meant to say.

Meanwhile Mary came with a glass of water, and raised him, and held it to his mouth. He drank quickly and greedily. While she was filling the glass again, he said: 'That water—ah—bad water.'

'There's salt in it,' she said, giving him more. 'You need salt in your body, so Rocky says. You'll probably not be well for a few days yet.'

All the while he gasped and swallowed. 'Bad water,' he said, when the glass was empty. 'Not just salt.' Nevertheless, he went on to drink two more glasses of it, before lying back, panting, on the pillows.

'Where is this?' he asked, later.

'This is Tourmaline,' Deborah said.

'Tourmaline.' He made a curious sound, like a laugh. 'I didn't think—ever——'

'Were you coming here?' she asked him.

Ah, yes—maybe. I didn't think——' He opened his eyes again and looked at me, down at the foot of the bed.

'I am the Law,' I said. 'Would you like to tell us who you are?'

He shifted his shoulders, uncomfortably, watching me all this time. At last: 'I'm not——' he said; and then, sighing: 'I'm—ah—diviner.'

32

'Diviner,' Deborah said, wondering.

'Dowser. Water. You know?' And his voice had grown thin and unsure.

But what a bound of my heart there was, to think that it was this that we had saved for Tourmaline. A diviner in our midst, in our waterless and dying town.

'A diviner,' Mary said. And she too was rapt.

'I'm—ah—tired,' he murmured. 'Sick. Could sleep some more.' But his half-open eyes had turned towards the door, and I looked round and saw Byrne leaning there, intent.

'A diviner, Byrnie,' Mary said. 'Imagine.'

He came to stand beside me at the bed's foot, and it seemed as if he couldn't take his black eyes from those blue ones. In time he said: 'Good day, mate.'

The diviner said nothing.

'You don't remember me,' Byrne said, 'do you?'

'Stranger,' the diviner said. 'First time—in Tourmaline.' He looked uneasy, suddenly, his eyes uncertain.

'You talked to me last night. Don't worry, you didn't say anything.'

'Sick,' said the diviner. 'Too much sun. Out of water.'

'And you a diviner,' said Byrne.

The man on the bed closed his eyes and sighed, painfully.

Byrne said: 'I wasn't getting at you. Honest. Anyone in this town's your mate. You staying with us?'

The diviner made a sound, a sort of audible shrug.

'We don't know your name, even,' Byrne said. He had taken charge of the proceedings. 'Well, this is the Law, up

33

here with me. That's Mary Spring next to you, it's her house you're in. Deborah over there's been nursing you, and I've been doing the same. I'm Bill Byrne.'

I recall that the rest of us were mildly surprised by this reminder that he had a Christian name. He had been Byrnie most of his life.

'But we don't know your name,' he persisted.

The diviner shifted and sighed on his pillows.

At length he murmured: 'Michael,' wearily.

'Good enough name,' Byrne said. And I remember thinking how oddly in command of himself he was that morning, how assured. His ravaged face was almost stern. 'That all?'

The diviner stirred.

'It doesn't matter, son.'

'Random,' said the diviner, suddenly, and as if he had surprised himself. And I knew then, we all knew, that he was lying.

Still, it was of no importance. We were only amused to see how little he knew of Tourmaline if he thought that his real name, for good or ill, could ever have reached us.

'Well,' said Byrne, 'I'm glad to know you, Mike.' And we all made small friendly noises. It was ludicrous. The diviner, in return, tortured himself into producing a smile.

'I'm glad—to be here,' he painfully informed us; and as it sounded so perfectly inane he went on to an equally painful but quite spontaneous laugh, in which we were relieved to join. It did serve to clear the air a bit.

'You'll soon be well,' Deborah said, coming closer to the bed.

'Yes,' he agreed. 'Soon.'

'But your poor face,' Mary said, 'it's going to come off in strips.'

'My face,' he echoed. 'Not worth much. Start with—a clean skin.'

He sounded exhausted, and I suppose had not noticed poor Byrnie's pits and craters, although he was looking directly at him as he spoke. The strain of making new acquaintances and attempting to be affable must have been, at that time, almost intolerable, and I began to feel guilty. We had leapt upon him like eager and loving dogs. He could not possibly know how much he meant to us.

Mary must have felt the same way; for she abruptly stopped studying him, and said: 'Everyone out of this room,' in a tone of command. 'You too, Deborah. Let him sleep in peace.'

So we were herded away; not without reluctance, in spite of our goodwill to the patient. The last to go was Byrne, who appeared to be laying claim to some special interest in our find (I say 'find' because no one apparently considered at that stage that the rights of ownership in our disputed property might be vested in the property himself) on the grounds of their earlier conversation. He leaned over the bed-end and said, rather wistfully: 'See you, Mike.'

'See you,' said the diviner, closing his eyes, 'ah—Jack.'

Poor Byrnie came out of the room looking rejected.

But outside in the store Tom was sitting, as usual, behind the counter. And for certain people (people, so far as I could see, who were bent on wrecking their lives, or had done so, like Jack Speed's father) he had a wonderfully warm and gentle smile. Byrne was one of them. I was moved to see that smile, and Byrne responding. I am soft at the heart, I know, soft at the heart; and they are so ghostly to me, all my fellow men, that such moments, when the reality of them is suddenly there, and brilliant, made manifest by one to another, and by both to me—such moments touch my soft old heart with a pleasure and pain past bearing. There stood poor Byrnie, wearing his twenty-eight years as if they had been eighty, there was so little in his life of hope and promise; and there was elderly Tom, bathing him in the radiance of his young smile. For a moment Byrne looked beautiful.

'He's a diviner,' he told Tom, elated.

'I knew,' said Tom, 'he was something—not common.'

'You haven't heard him yet.'

'I'll wait,' Tom said. 'The boy's weak still.'

I went away from them, leaving them talking. I went to my house and spoke, as on every other morning, to the wireless. Why did I think, listening to the silence, of our wild garden at home, and of tough frail lilies breaking open the ground, before the earliest rains?

THREE

Then for three days we saw nothing of him, although from Mary we had a running commentary on his activities. He was deeply depressed, we heard, and would lie on his bed all day without moving. He suffered from headaches, and from fits of shivering, during which the sweat poured from him, leaving him cold as a fish. His skin began to peel. On the third day he shaved himself, taking off a good deal of his epidermis with the hair. His proportions had returned to normal, but Mary found herself unable to form any aesthetic judgement on his face, which, she said, most resembled the flaking ceilings of the Tourmaline Hotel; although not (she added, with a hiss of insecticide) held together with the vomit of flies.

Byrne fretted, kept unjustly at a distance from his interesting property; to whom, it seemed to us, he had been inexplicably bullying and tedious, and who probably

37

did not care to see him again. On the second night he got drunk, and sang for several hours from his usual platform. Later he staggered into the bar and made a long oration to Kestrel on the subject of the diviner, during which the phrase 'The desert'll blossom' occurred many times. Kestrel replied, when he could: 'Will you get out of here?' Byrne then offered to go and live with Jack Speed's father, at his camp ten miles away, and never set foot in Tourmaline again, if that was Kestrel's desire. After that Kestrel and Rock laid hands on him, and dragged him off to his bed.

On the first night or two of the diviner's sojourn in Tourmaline Kestrel's attitude to him was charitably neutral. By the fourth night he hated him. He had not, of course, seen him since a few minutes after his arrival, and he was not so rash as to pass any judgement; but when Michael Random's name was mentioned, the set of his mouth said all that was needed. Said more, indeed, if he had known, than he may have wished; for there were not many people in Tourmaline who did not guess pretty early that he was afraid of the diviner. I think he saw himself deserted, bereft of Deborah, and of Byrne; such a charm the other man seemed to have, even when insensible.

Deborah was more silent than ever. But one afternoon, not long after a quarrel, I suspect, she took a first sip of some tea she had made, and grimaced, and said to Kestrel: 'You've been here all your life, and what have you given us? Rum.'

There was no water, he told her. Did she think no one had tried? Did she think Tourmaline hadn't enough cranks of its own, without picking them up off the road?

She said nothing, to great effect.

Rock was stolidly hopeful. For many years, even before it was his, the meagre garden had been kept alive with the waste water and kitchen slops of the whole town, and this had to be collected. The rest thought first of the gold. In the bar of the hotel, with Kestrel dourly watching, visions arose of a Tourmaline greater and richer even than in its heyday, a town paved with gold and murmuring with sluices, inhabited solely by millionaires. So wild was the optimism that there seemed to be a hazy feeling that the drought might break with the diviner's coming, and the millionaires go yachting on Lake Tourmaline.

This was the state of hope and curiosity he induced in us. And on the fifth day of his citizenship, having been informed by Mary of our mounting impatience, he sent word that he was ready to be visited.

Mary's sitting room, furnished with cane and seagrass chairs, and dominated by a panoramic photograph of Tourmaline in its prosperity, now brown and nearly featureless, was a bleak place, but cool; cooler, certainly, than the more comfortable parts of the hotel, with their monstrosities of brown velvet and imitation leather. No fly ever intruded there, and very little light, for the aged green curtains were always drawn. An upright piano (the property, need I say, of Tom's grandmother) glimmered in one corner, surmounted by a silver lamp. The carpet, originally green, but worn bare in many places, resembled a drought-stricken lawn. In another corner stood a bookcase, containing the pick of the Miners' Institute's one thousand volumes, and as much wisdom, I dare say, as there was to be found in Tourmaline, in those days or in ours.

It was into this room that Mary led me, and after me Byrne, to be received by the diviner.

He had been lounging in an ancient basket-chair, but rose to meet us as Mary pushed back the door, looking self-conscious, I noticed. Tom had dressed him in blue dungarees, with a blue shirt, such as most of us wear, and as he faced into the light that fell through the open door I was struck again by the deep cloudy colour of his eyes, like the Timor Sea, as I remember it, long ago. Something about him always recalled to me the sea, the coast, many things I have not known since I was young. There was so much hope in the look of him.

He was moderately tall, I discovered, about an inch under six feet, a good manageable size. In height and build, indeed, he was almost the double of Byrne, and in his first days at Tourmaline they were often confused. Both were thin, sinewy, almost hipless, with that apparently spindly but actually unbreakable wiriness that the plants of these arid regions also have. Even in his prostration we had seen that he was tough; and that in spite of the fact that the ribs showed under his skin like the laths of a crumbling wall.

All this time I had been studying him, in the way he must by then have been getting used to, and beginning to hate. But he came forward pleasantly enough, and shook hands with me. Curious hands he had; rather fine, strong hands, but seeming somehow to consist of not much more than his fine, strong bones, elusive and ungraspable.

This was emphasized by his still being coated with unguents, although no longer with the whitish prepara-tion with which Mary had first plastered him. He gleamed wherever his skin was exposed. His straight nose shone like a plum. Threads of skin clung to his lips, and he did in general, as Mary had said, resemble the flaking ceilings of Kestrel's pub.

Even so, it was evident that he possessed certain advantages. He had fine bones, and the yellow hair flopped over his forehead in an amiable way. If he had good looks, they were of a kind that could irritate nobody. In a word, he was prepossessing.

I said that I was pleased to see him so well.

'I've been lucky,' he said. 'Lucky to land in a place like this. Mary and Tom have treated me like a son, or something.'

Byrne had been standing behind me, dark and expectant, like a shy dog gauging a stranger. The diviner presented his lean hand.

'Thanks for looking after me,' he said.

Byrne suddenly grinned like the sun. 'You did remember.'

'Not that part of it. But thanks, anyway.' And then he hung irresolate, and it became apparent how severe a trial he found all this sociable behaviour, probably wishing us at the devil all the while.

'You're a mystery to us,' I said, to take the burden of conversation off his shoulders. 'How could a man be found fifty miles from Tourmaline, and not even a bicycle beside him?'

He turned aside, rubbing his peeling forehead with his wrist, nervily. Then: 'D'you mind if I sit down?' he asked, laying his loose bones in the basket-chair. We did not, and sat too. 'I walked,' he said at last.

'You walked,' I repeated. It sounded insane.

'What a man,' sighed Byrne, who was disposed to worship this enigma in any case.

'Only at night,' the diviner explained. 'For the first ten days, that is.'

'But you had no water,' I said.

'I had a bag,' he said. 'Where is it? In the truck, maybe. Or maybe I threw it away.'

'It was empty, then. Well, of course, after ten days.'

'I don't need much,' he said, 'and I depended on, you know, finding some on the way. I have a—a gift, in that line. I'm a diviner, did I tell you?'

I remarked that everyone in Tourmaline now knew of it, and looked to him for salvation. He frowned, under his yellow forelock.

'But you didn't find any water,' Byrne suggested. 'This is hard country, son.'

'I know it,' he said. 'But no country's hopeless. Only, I lost my rod, a metal rod—you know? And nothing else would do. When that was gone, the—the virtue went out of me. And I was sick...'

'What the hell did you eat?' Byrne wondered.

'I took as many tins as I could carry. I don't need much, you see.

'You don't drink and you don't eat,' Byrne said. 'Have a smoke, for Christ's sake, you make us uncomfortable.' He proffered his tobacco tin, and the diviner, after looking at his face, hesitantly, took it and rolled a cigarette. 'Anyway,' Byrne went on, 'tell us what happened after those ten days. How long was it before the bloke found you?'

42

'Two days,' the diviner said, 'I think. But I was pretty crook by that time.'

'You're telling me you were.'

'The day before, I woke up about night-time, I found I'd been sleeping all day in the open sun. Face swelled up like a football—you saw it—and not quite right in the head, either.'

He lit his cigarette. I noticed that his hand trembled. 'Are you cold, still?' I asked him.

'No,' he said, 'no, only—I'm often like this. Anyway, I kept walking all that night, and then I kept on in the morning, because things were looking—not too good, you know, and I reckoned I'd have to get here quick or not get here at all. But the sun sort of knocked me down on the road. Couldn't do anything. Crawled under a bit of bush that let the sun in on me and just lay there. After that, I don't remember much, except a bloke pulling me around, and then—then, the heat of that truck.' He shivered, hunching his shoulders. 'I thought I was in hell,' he said, sincerely.

Byrne's black eyes were fascinated by him. I too was absorbed, but troubled by certain rents in his costume of gallant folly, behind which he remained unchanged and indecipherable.

'You've gone through a lot,' I said, 'and you've told us a lot. But after all that, we still don't know why anyone would want to walk to Tourmaline.'

He leaned back, closing his eyes, and directing a jet of smoke at the centre of the room. I saw that I had disturbed him. But he answered, after a minute's silence: 'It was here. That's all.'

43

'You'd heard of us, then?'

'Oh, in a roundabout way. I'd heard of some towns that were supposed to be—well, relics. And Tourmaline was one of them. I don't suppose it'd hurt your feelings if I said that no one cares a cracker whether the place is still here or not. In fact, most people think it's been dead for years.'

'That was Lacey's Find,' Byrne said. 'The sand blew up and buried it.'

'A buried town.' The diviner thought about it, dreamily, and with a curious yearning intensity.

I too was remembering, not for the first time, the broad street of Lacey's, the two-storied hotel, the several stores. I imagined the gentle tidal encroachment of the dunes, the soft red sand, wind-ribbed and untrodden, mounting, mounting. Over the bar of the hotel, over the piano and the billiard table, over the counters and merchandise of the stores; until, in the end, what would be left but a chimney or two of the hotel, dully moaning in the red wind? And those too, of course, the wind would have silenced by now, and the sand would lie unbroken and printless over all the places that knew me. In my terrible loneliness I grow elegiac.

'I've made a song about it,' Byrne said. 'Or about Tourmaline—about the same thing happening to Tourmaline. It's not far from here to the dune country. Just keep on going through the broken fence, and keep an eye open for Leichardt.'

'I've finished walking,' said the diviner, with his absent and innocent grin. 'I'll stay here.'

'That's good news,' said Byrne, returning it.

I got up and went to the bookcase, feeling that at this

important moment the diviner must be initiated into the history and condition of our heritage. I fetched the massive *Cyclopedia of Western Australia* (the property of Tom's grandfather) and read to him the account of our town in its heyday. Like unto those of fabled Ophir (I informed him) were the riches and future prospects of Tourmaline, so recently a trackless wilderness. Where once reigned desolation was now a prosperous town, containing all the comforts and facilities of a city. The streets, two chains in width, were well illumined with acetylene gas, and the principal thoroughfares planted with pepper trees. The town possessed, besides a telephone exchange and the usual government buildings, a hospital, a miners' institute (containing nearly 1,000 volumes) and several churches. The religious life was strong and vigorous. There was an excellent volunteer fire-brigade. The town was also the place of publication of the principal newspaper of the district, the *Tourmaline Times*, which enjoyed a wide circulation and popularity. The population, in spite of an inadequate water supply, had risen to 900. There was weekly communication by coach with Lacey's Find and other centres. In point of view of its many facilities, this outpost of civilization could vie with many older established communities; and indeed (so I read) it far distanced some in the race for progress.

When I had concluded this lesson, I carried the book to him and let him gaze upon the photograph of Tourmaline in its pride, the main street thronged with stores and pepper trees, a handsome street lamp prominent in the centre foreground. I don't know why, but the town was deserted except for a black dog on its way across the road.

He looked at it, smiling faintly, and then glanced through the encomium I had just read him. Suddenly he burst out into a bubbling laugh.

I was bitterly disappointed. I am not humourless, I hope, but the splendour of Tourmaline is not a laughing matter. Still shaking, he went on to ask: 'Does the—does the volunteer fire-brigade still function?'

'In case of fire,' Byrne said, 'every able-bodied man drops what he's doing, rushes to the scene of the conflagration and pisses on it. On account of there's a water shortage, mate.'

Again the laugh bubbled up; infectious, and very youthful. I could not be displeased.

'You're a crude beast, Byrnie,' said Deborah from the door. 'I'm ashamed of you.' And she did manage to look severe as she came into the room, so that Byrne blushed, as she had intended he should. He was very modest with women.

We stood up for her. The diviner took her tawny hand and thanked her for her kindness to him in his extremity.

She rested her fathomless gaze on his face. And again I had the impression that he was uneasy, on his guard, with her as with Byrne; and yet with the Springs, with me, there was no hint of such constraint. And I remarked to myself that he seemed to be a diviner of less tangible things than water.

'You're famous now,' she said. 'The most famous man in Tourmaline. It's good to see you looking so well.'

'I've got you and Mary to thank for that,' he said. 'And Byrnie for my fame, I reckon. Mary tells me it was your husband who saved me from flattening my face on the street out there.'

She turned aside to sit down, and murmured: 'Fancy Mary speaking well of Kes.'

'Is that speaking well of him?'

'In a way. He wouldn't do much to save Mary from flattening her face.'

'Deb,' said Byrne, 'he doesn't want to hear this.' That Kestrel should be disparaged was a blow at whatever shreds he himself possessed of confidence and self-esteem.

'Will he come here?' the diviner asked her.

'Kes? No, never. He's scared of Mary.'

'Kes is all right,' Byrne hastened to explain. 'She's joking. He did get you out of the truck. Him and the Law, there. He's okay.'

'You'll find Tourmaline a funny place,' I said. 'People like each other. There's a lot of what we used to call esprit de corps.'

'Like in the days of the volunteer fire-brigade,' Byrne put in; with intent, I suppose, to mock me, but the diviner did not respond.

'In spite of what Deborah says,' I added (portentously, I need not confess), 'Kestrel has a great regard for Mary. Tourmaline's like that.'

'A funny place, all right,' the diviner said; and I could not tell from his tone whether he was impressed or covertly amused. But he must have known, behind those blue hills, terrible things. He must have been acquainted, as we are not, with the danger—the terrible danger—that danger of which I know nothing, but which drives me night and

47

morning to prayer, and fills my sleep with images of wind and annihilation.

'Do you come from the coast?' I was impelled to ask him. 'You're a seaman, perhaps?'

'No,' he said. 'A seaman? Never.' And would say no more, then or ever.

'Where do you come from then?' Byrne asked.

'From the other end of the road,' he said; and smiled, evasively. 'Where else could I come from?'

'And what's there?' asked Deborah. It is the women, always, who are most curious about that road.

He sat twisting in his lap the fingers of his multi-coloured hands, and studying them. Then he said, rather quietly: 'Hell.'

And I felt cold. No one would speak. He meant it.

'You seem to believe in hell,' I said at length, for he oppressed us too much with his sincerity. 'That's rare.'

He shrugged. 'In Tourmaline, maybe.'

'We're innocent, I suppose.'

'More than I ever hoped for.' He spoke very softly.

All the while Deborah and Byrne were gazing at him, much as children used to stare at Ah Quong the Chinaman. It must have been trying.

'Tom has told me a lot about the place,' he said; and I tried to determine what Tom, who was so religiously word-less, could have found to tell, and how much he had observed in his hermit-existence, and whether his observations might not contain elements which had escaped the rest of us. 'I've never met a man like Tom. I've never struck a town like this. Maybe there aren't any more. I could believe it.'

'You sound as if you'd never had a home,' said Deborah.

'No,' he said, shortly. 'Out there——' Then he stopped for a moment, but meeting her eyes for the first time went on, with a sort of despairing candour: 'I'm not the kind, you see. It's—ah, chaos. Like nothing here. Tom couldn't live. I couldn't live. D'you understand?' And suddenly he was far younger, terribly eager that we should understand, that we should acquit him—but of what? Again he appeared to me obscure, alien.

'And the man who drives the truck?'

'Is a saint, a crazy saint. So they say.'

'That bastard?' Byrne said, incredulous.

'It's different,' he said, 'out there.'

'You mustn't tell us,' I said suddenly. Because I was afraid. Because of the danger—the terrible danger. It was as if my silent wireless had finally spoken, and for Tourmaline's sake I must clap my hands to my ears, and close my mind, and hear nothing—nothing—but the gathering wind, perhaps, and the slow soft hush of sand at every door.

'Wild beasts are loose on the world,' he said, from another place, as it were. 'When you know that, you don't need to know much more.'

But Tom, who had come into the room, unnoticed, said: 'Don't you?' And as the diviner turned to look at him the luminous smile transfigured his lean face and Random's equally. 'This room's full of wild beasts, too, that might be let loose at any moment. The question is, what controls them?'

'You know,' the diviner said, with great trust and happiness.

49

And Tom wondered: 'Do I? Because it might be just a kid's convention, mightn't it? What if the Word was only 'Barleys', after all?'

The diviner stared into his eyes, and the light went out of him. He said, or rather queried: 'You're fooling, Tom.'

'Tom, Tom,' I pleaded with him, 'don't destroy what you can't build again.'

'If I believed that,' the diviner said, 'I couldn't live.' And he gave to this most grotesque of conversation-killers an awful force and solemnity.

'Don't stop at the first gate, Mike,' Tom gently said. 'It's not a substitute for thinking.' And he stood with his back to the edge of the open door, swaying himself back and forth a little, as he looked down, luminous, on the young man. He was very thin, and somehow shrunken, although I don't remember that he was ever larger. Deep lines ascended his forehead and almost overtook the receding hair. Even so, the impression he gave was of youth; an impression reinforced by the youthful timbre of his voice, and by a certain diffident and respectful quality in his smile.

'Then what's your belief?' asked the diviner, blind to the rest of us.

'I'm still waiting,' Tom said. 'Who'd dare say before the end of the road?' And with his hands behind him, palms to the flat of the door, he swayed himself.

The diviner lolled in his basket-chair, limp. I remembered his phrase before, speaking of the loss of his divining rod. 'The virtue went out of me.' He looked like that.

'What's it matter, anyway?' Byrne demanded. 'We'll live till we die. Who gives a stuff about beliefs?'

'We'll live till we die,' Tom echoed. 'If we believe we exist, that's enough.'

'It's not enough,' Deborah said, 'not if you just believe that you exist. You have to believe that Mary exists, or Byrnie, or someone. You've got to believe it in your guts.' And what startled me was not so much her apparent reading of my thoughts as the ferocity with which she spoke, the bitterness in her. Poor girl, I thought; Kestrel has broken her heart.

'Ah, Deb,' Tom said, 'won't you come home?'

'I've made my bed,' she said; and laughed. 'My good old double bed with the brass knobs. I'll lie in it.'

'Kes is all right,' said Byrne, forlornly.

'D'you think he believes *you* exist?'

'How do I know? I can't even understand what you buggers are talking about.'

'You think he treats you like a brother,' she said. 'Well, he does, too. Like a brother to Jock'—meaning Kestrel's black mongrel. 'Except that Jock doesn't drink his grog.'

'Stop it, Deb,' Tom said, unsmiling.

'He brought me up,' Byrne protested (it was terrible, it was harrowing to watch him). 'From the time I was thirteen. Tom——'

The girl put her hand up, wearily, to her hair, which was tied behind with a strip of blue cloth, and did something to it without noticing. Her small breasts showed sharp under the blue dress. Her eyes were on the carpet and her full lips drawn in.

'Oh Byrnie,' she said, 'I'm sorry. I'm sorry, I'm sorry. Poor boy...'

51

'You must hate him,' he accused her. 'Why don't you leave him? Is it fair, do you reckon?'

'No, I don't,' she said, sombrely. 'I don't hate him. I'm the biggest fool of all.' She rose as she spoke, and looked towards the diviner. 'I'm sorry,' she said again. 'This isn't what you thought we were like.'

He glanced up, absently, with eyes that had grown sullen. 'It's nothing,' he said. 'Don't worry about me.'

'I hope you'll come to the pub and meet him.'

'Yes,' he said vaguely. 'I'll do that. Goodbye, Mrs—ah, Kestrel.'

She was taken aback by that. So were we all. It sounded like someone else's name. But she smiled after a moment, and turned away to Tom.

'Must go home, Pa,' she said to him.

'So that's home,' he said, 'is it? Ah well.'

She dropped a gentle kiss on him and went out.

When she had gone, Byrne stretched out his long legs. Then he scratched himself, intimately. Then he said, in an injured tone: 'She reckons she's doing him a big favour. Who does she think she is?'

'Shut up, Byrnie,' said Tom.

He took no offence, but continued to glower at the piano. 'I'm mixed up,' said the diviner, with a sigh.

'Come and have a drink,' said Byrne, but with no particular eagerness.

'Not now,' the diviner said. 'Thanks.'

'Perhaps you'd like to see the town,' I hoped.

He beat on his knee with the flat of his hand, irritably. 'My head's cracking open,' he complained. 'Oh hell. Tom——'

'I'll get you something in a minute.'

'I didn't know the girl was your daughter.'

'She's not,' Tom said. 'Well, foster-daughter.'

'They don't seem very happy across the road.'

All of a sudden he had deteriorated, had become querulous, like an invalid. He made this last comment fretfully, as if the fact were an injury. The peeling forehead was knitted with pain above the resentful eyes. I felt that he meant us to leave him, and prepared to go quite gladly because, I discovered, I didn't care for him. He was no longer prepossessing.

'Are you crook again?' Byrne enquired, with excessive sympathy.

'My head,' he said, sounding confused. 'Doesn't matter, just get worse, got to expect it.' He put his hands up to his eyes, and kept on muttering in muffled tones from behind them. 'Have to stop thinking, that's all. Could have been dead, anything else is pure gain.'

Byrne looked at me, at a loss, and then at Tom, who removed his spine from the edge of the door and went out. In a moment he returned with a glass of water and a couple of tablets, which the diviner took and swallowed without opening his eyes. Then for a while the room was still.

'I'm off,' Byrne said at last, getting up. I rose too.

'Sorry,' the diviner murmured. 'Some other time.' But as we passed through the door he called out: 'Byrnie.'

Byrne responded like a sheepdog.

'My rod,' the diviner said. 'Tom said you might make one. Can you?'

'Sure,' Byrne said. 'In the forge up at the mine. Glad to do it.'

This he need not have said, for he looked like the recipient of some outstanding honour as it was. But the diviner had his eyes closed.

'Good bloke,' said the diviner, weakly, and relapsed into the self-absorption of his pain. So we went out, Byrne and I. But we heard, as we entered the shop, his voice rising to ask Tom some question, and Tom's replying, with irony and compassion.

FOUR

In the morning, feeling aimless, I came out of my back door and wandered across a stretch of bare red earth to the gaol; my gaol, to which I am constantly returning, the shrine and the museum of law in Tourmaline. Against the intense blue of the Tourmaline sky, the walls of the exercise yard, like a low square tower, glimmered with all the light and purity the sun could discover in their pale stonework; and I noticed again, with pride, the rough beauty of the round window set high in the front wall, the handsome curve of masonry above the gate. The wooden door that used to cover that gate has fallen from its hinges and lies, cracked and blistered, in the open sun. The gate, lightly filmed with rust, cried out as I put my shoulder to its resistance.

In the yard, nothing has changed for many years. The long cell facing the entrance is unroofed now, and the wall around its doorway has collapsed, covering the floor with rubble. An odd collection of old basins, bits of harness, branding irons, ledgers and journals and papers, buries the paving of the yard to a depth of about a foot. I squatted in the cool shadow, luminous with reflected light from the walls, and began to read a report, in brown ink, of the disappearance of a box of gold between Lacey's Find and Tourmaline. The affair was mysterious, and I had my suspicions of the constable who recounted it. But I couldn't help liking him for his generous commendations of P/H (or Police Horse) Rory.

While I was reading, a shadow came across the light from the gateway, and I looked round and saw Byrne there, watching me. He was returning from his second home, the hut on the hill, and had seen me go into the gaol.

'What've you got there?' he asked, idly, standing over me.

I showed him. He glanced at the pages, but quickly lost interest. And I remembered that reading was something of an effort to him.

'I'm going to see Mike,' he said. 'About the rod.'

'You're making it, then?'

'When he'll come and show me. I don't know what he wants. I thought they used a bit of bush, but he doesn't.'

'He's a very serious young man,' I suggested.

'He doesn't muck about,' Byrne agreed, looking very spindly and drought-stricken as he stood there among the high walls.

'Come with us,' he invited.

'No,' I said, 'it's a long hot walk to the mine. I'll stay and dig about in this.'

He looked down at me, with his bright black eyes,

like a clever sheepdog's. 'You're getting an old man,' he remarked, as if he had never observed this before, and thought I too might be interested to know. 'I forgot that.'

'I forget it myself,' I confessed, rummaging among the papers. 'But there's plenty to remind me—especially in here.' I went on, as I spoke, to flip through the pages of an ancient police gazette from New Zealand, studying the interesting faces of long-ago felons; but I was aware that as I did so he stood, with thumbs in his belt and long head on one side, studying me. The thought had come to him, I suddenly knew, that I must die. And what will become of Tourmaline then, he wonders.

I scanned the sad features of one Timaru Joe (robbery with violence) and waited for Byrne to follow up the painful topic. But on this one day he seemed less inclined to pass on the first thought that came into his head; there was even an air of conscious tactfulness about him, as he stood over me, which depressed me profoundly, and drove me to say at last: 'You're wondering who'll come after me when I'm gone.'

But to my intense humiliation, he replied: 'What's it matter?' I had misread him, utterly.

'I am the law,' I said, as humbly as such an assertion could well be made; for I meant by it, the memory and the conscience of Tourmaline. 'Grant that to an old man.'

He looked at me with pity—with genuine pity, I swear it. It was too much, too much to bear. 'But there's Kes,' he said. 'And Tom, and Rocky. And Jack at the mine. And now Mike. What do you want?'

'The law,' I said. 'The memory.' But I could not express myself to him. He was young, and would have interpreted my sentiments as senile conceit, as a mere frightened fist-shaking in the face of nothingness. In the bright cool shade of the stone yard I felt alone and threatened, as if abandoned, by night, on the great shelterless plains through which the diviner had passed to come to Tourmaline.

'You'll live forever,' he said kindly. 'Don't worry.' Because he himself had discovered hope, only a few days ago, he could patronize me, flying his brand-new purpose from the masthead. He was absurd, but also touching.

'Bless you, Byrnie,' I murmured, with an irony not ill-intentioned. 'I can manage to keep on.'

He grinned, moving back into the gateway. 'I'll go and see Mike,' he said, 'and get this rod sorted out. And then you'll see what's going to become of Tourmaline.' His blue figure, with a kind of salute, stepped out into the sunlight. 'See you,' he called back, and vanished around my walls, making for the road.

I squatted, meanwhile, in my cool light well, deciphering a letter from a lady of Geraldton, who demanded with some force that her ex-de facto husband be compelled to contribute to the maintenance of the child he had inflicted on her. Her style was terse and embittered. She appeared to upbraid my predecessor, to indict in him all members of our sex. I was a long time pondering over this letter, which pleased me with its wealth of domestic detail, and in unearthing other documents of a later date, some of them in my own writing.

So the morning passed away. And poor Byrnie, denied admission to the diviner, who was indisposed, settled down in the hotel to get drunk.

*

That evening he was singing, as usual, on the war memorial, his reformation already a thing of the past, apparently. Deborah came out to speak to him, kind but disapproving. He was far gone by then, and began to weep, abjectly, clutching his guitar and staring straight at her, like a child. She said: 'Poor Byrnie,' and went away again.

Inside the pub, Horse Carson, who was also drunk, was having an argument with Kestrel. Horse's bark face was slightly flushed, but not, of course, animated—nothing could have made that eroded, deep-channelled plain less immobile. But he gestured now and then with his mallee-root fists, and seemed concerned to prove something.

'Would you throw the poor bugger back again?' he demanded of Kestrel. 'Is that the kind of bastard you are? You ought to be driving that truck yourself, by Jesus.'

'Did I say that?' Kestrel asked, in his curiously soft voice.

'What did you say, well?'

'That he ought to go back where he came from. What's he want here? We don't need him.'

'"We don't need him,"' Horse quoted, with scorn. 'Ah no, mate. We don't need water. We got rum to wash gold in. If we ever feel like a shower, we can always come down here and get you to tip a bottle over us. What would we want with water?'

'There isn't any water,' Kestrel said, with an edge.

'So we got your word for it,' Horse said. 'When did you set up as a dowser?'

'Look, d'you think no other silly bastard's ever tried?'

'This bloke's no ordinary silly bastard,' Horse affirmed.

'This bloke's something special. You only got to look at him.'

'Ah hell,' said Kestrel in disgust. 'Rocky, talk a bit of sense into him.'

'What makes you so sure he's no good?' Rock wondered. He was standing, sad and sober, beside Horse, and gazing into his drink, which he did not seem to want. 'He's the sort of bloke who might know something. I'd trust him. I'd even pay him to try his hand at it, if that was what he was after. But he isn't, by the looks of it. He just wants to stay here.'

'He'll be a social asset, all right,' Kestrel said. 'One of Mary's mob—a man with religion.'

'Ah, so what?' Horse said. 'You don't drink now, do you? Everyone's got some little virtue that craps someone else to death.'

'Lay off, Horse,' Jack Speed said.

'I'll lay off when Kes lays off the new bloke,' Horse replied.

In the meantime Byrne had come in, trailing his guitar, and had pushed himself in between Horse and Rock. 'Give us a drink?' he asked Kestrel.

'You've had a bellyful,' his cousin said. 'Go and ask your mate for a bucket of water.'

'Buy me a drink, Horse.'

'Sure,' said Horse, who had credit (in gold) with Kestrel. 'Give the poor sod a glass.'

'You're a bludger,' Kestrel said to Byrne.

'Yair,' said Byrne. 'Makes you thirsty, don't it?'

'Bludge off me then,' Kestrel said coldly. 'Not off your mates. I'll make sure you work for it.'

'Okay, okay,' said Byrne, 'I'll bludge off you, Kes. Keep it in the family.' But he helped himself, absent-mindedly, to Rock's glass while he was waiting.

'Kes doesn't think too highly of the bloke across the road,' Jack Speed said.

'He's a good bloke,' Byrne asserted, rather slurred in his speech by this time.

'Who, Kes?'

'Kes is a good bloke,' said Byrne, sentimentally. 'Mike's a good bloke. We're all good blokes, all us bastards. Horse's a good bloke, now,' he further particularized, putting his arm round Horse's shoulders and leaning on him heavily. 'He's a real good bloke, old Horse. I like you, you old bastard.'

'Yair, well, get off of me,' Horse said, removing himself.

Byrne staggered a little. 'Mike's crook again,' he rambled on, in his drunken monotone. 'He gets these headaches. Will he be like that all the time, d'you reckon, Rocky?'

'How do I know?' Rock said. 'Could be.'

'Hope he gets over it. He's a good bloke, that one.'

'You seem to have said that,' remarked Kestrel.

'Don't be that way, Kes.'

'I'm sick of the sound of this joker,' Kestrel confessed. 'But what the hell. He hasn't done anything to me.'

Byrne belched, and drank, and then, still muttering something about good blokes, planted his elbow on the bar, forearm up. Horse did the same, and they grasped hands. Rock and Jack moved aside, as the struggle began, to see who could force down the other's arm; a long deadlock, tedious to watch, a commonplace event in that bar of Kestrel's. Byrne's tongue protruded with the effort. Horse's face was red.

'That's his drinking arm, Horse,' Kestrel said. 'See if you can break it.'

'Come on, Byrnie,' Jack Speed said, 'he'll have you in a minute.'

Byrne grunted in denial. He was right. Horse's elbow suddenly skidded in a pool of liquor, and he went staggering away, to land, after some complicated manoeuvres designed to preserve his balance, on the floor. Byrne gripped the bar and stood panting.

'I won,' he claimed.

'Like hell you did,' Horse growled from the floor. 'That wasn't a fair contest.'

'Replay,' ordered Rock, the universal umpire.

'Here,' said Horse, 'on the floor. Can't fall then.' He rolled over on his stomach and put his arm up. So Byrne lay down, facing him, and the battle resumed. But as they were no longer in anyone's way, no one troubled to watch it.

In any case, it didn't last long, owing to another diversion. For Kestrel, who was talking to Rock, suddenly looked up from his forefinger tracing wet patterns on the bar, and fixed his pale grey eyes on the doorway. And there, politely hesitating, was the diviner.

They looked at one another for awhile. No one but Kestrel had seen him. They just stood there, learning each other's faces.

Then: 'Come in,' Kestrel called to him; and everyone turned about.

'It's him,' said Rock, as if to make quite sure that the

62

diviner knew they had been talking about him. 'Come over.' He made a place for him at the bar.

'It's Mike,' Byrne shouted, scrambling up from the floor. 'Thought you were crook.'

'I'm okay,' said the diviner. But his voice was subdued and weary. He stood beside Rock, one elbow on the bar, and looked at Kestrel. 'I came to say thanks,' he said.

'Don't thank me,' Kestrel said, offhand. 'I haven't done a thing.'

'I hear you were going to take me on, only Mary grabbed me.' It was strange what a tone of humility, of shame, almost, his voice acquired whenever he spoke of the manner of his coming to Tourmaline. 'It was a nice thought.'

'I'm full of them,' Kestrel said. 'Like, have a drink.'

'I'll buy him a drink,' Byrne offered.

'You've made a friend in the village idiot,' Kestrel said. 'Listen to him.'

'It's on me,' Rock said.

'It's on the house,' said Kestrel, bleakly, and poured a rum. I don't think anything else is drunk in Tourmaline. 'Get that down you. Better stuff than water.'

'Tourmaline water, anyway,' said the diviner, drinking with sober caution.

'Things are gunna change,' Horse called up happily from the floor, where he had made himself comfortable, apparently, and meant to stay. 'There's gunna be water in tankfuls.'

'Get me to the river Jordan,' said Kestrel, softly. 'You've made a lot of converts here.'

The diviner looked at him, and looked away again, uneasily. He was bewildered by this hostility, for which he could find no reason. It was hard for him, accepted everywhere as an unlucky invalid, the gallant victim of country not many would care to face, to understand that Kestrel actually mistrusted him. So he drank rather quickly, and the hand holding the thick glass trembled just a little. This Kestrel noticed, puzzled.

'When are you going to start work?' Rock asked, with carefully concealed hopefulness. 'Not right now, I dare say.'

'I don't know,' said the diviner, sounding confused. 'I don't know about going out in the bush—in the sun—now. And Byrnie's got to make me a rod yet.'

'I would have made it today,' Byrne reproached him, 'only you wouldn't let me in to ask you about it.'

The diviner painfully smiled. 'My head was bad,' he said.

'Get me a drink, Byrnie,' Horse called out. 'Let's drink to the water.'

'Yair,' said Rock, raising his glass, 'to the water.'

'To the water,' said Jack.

'To the water,' repeated the diviner; with a certain diffidence.

'Good luck,' said Kestrel, smiling crookedly. But as he had no glass he couldn't drink to it.

'Where's my bloody drink, Byrnie?'

'Hang on,' Byrne shouted. He lay down on the floor again, facing Horse. 'To the water,' they yelled in unison. Then they went back to their arm-bending contest, grunting and straining.

'Your wife's been pretty kind to me,' the diviner said, constrainedly.

'She's a good girl,' Kestrel agreed, with an expression-less face.

'She's a lot like Mary and Tom.'

'Yair,' said Kestrel. 'I can't cure her of it.'

After that the diviner looked so extremely uncom-fortable that even Kestrel was moved in the direction of sympathy, and went on: 'Don't get me wrong. I like Tom. I like Mary; but we have different ideas about most things.'

'Ah, yair,' murmured the diviner, twisting his glass about on the bar. 'Bound to.'

A shout of triumph came up from the floor, where Byrne had conquered Horse.

'Where you going to live?' Jack asked the diviner. 'At Tom's?'

'Don't think so,' the diviner said. 'Couldn't do that to them. I'll move in somewhere.'

'Plenty of empty houses,' Kestrel said. 'Something Tourmaline has got.'

'You're welcome at the mine,' Jack offered. 'I live up there. She's a good solid shack, got a bore with a drop of water in it.'

'Going to be water everywhere soon,' Horse remarked from the floor, where he was resting after his labours.

'I don't know yet,' said the diviner, answering Jack. 'But thanks for the offer. I can't,' he said, and hesitated, and went on with a nervous laugh, 'can't get used to Tourma-line, to the——You're bloody good people,' he concluded, in a rush.

'Have another drink,' Kestrel invited, rather crushingly ignoring this testimonial.

'No, you can't——' he protested, fumbling in his pocket. 'Let me shout. I've got some cash here.' And he dragged out his money, which most people already knew by sight, and put it on the bar. I don't think he realized at that time how thoroughly the town was acquainted with his person and property.

'He's a good bloke,' Byrne sang out. 'Good on you, Mike.' He staggered to his feet, swaying, and grabbed the diviner by the shoulder. The diviner winced.

'Get your gorilla's hands off the customers,' Kestrel said, without looking up from the bottle he was uncorking. 'Time we chucked you out, anyway.'

'Try it,' Byrne challenged, feeling tough after his tussle with Horse. He examined the diviner's arm as it rested on the bar. 'Good wrists you got,' he said. 'Want to take me on?

'At what?' asked the diviner.

'Arm-bending,' Byrne said, with his elbow firmly planted and his arm up, ready.

'Ah, no,' the diviner said. 'I'm drinking.'

'Go to buggery, will you,' said Kestrel. But Byrne ignored him.

'Come on,' he invited. 'What are you waiting for?'

So the diviner reluctantly put his arm up, and they grappled. There was a short straining silence; then a bit of a yelp from Byrne, and it was over.

'Satisfied?' Kestrel enquired. But he did not look pleased.

Byrne nursed his wrist. 'My elbow slipped,' he claimed. 'Replay.'

'It was okay,' Rock pronounced. 'Nick off, Byrnie.'

'Replay,' Byrne shouted. He was getting noisier. 'On the floor, Mike. Try it again.'

'To hell with that,' said the diviner. 'You may be drunk, but I'm not.'

'Horse,' Kestrel called, 'pull the silly bastard over and shut him up.' So Horse fastened his mallee-root hands on Byrne's ankle and dragged him down. And comparative peace followed while they wrestled.

'He's your cousin,' the diviner said, 'so he tells me.'

'It could happen to anyone,' said Kestrel.

'He seems to think a lot of you.'

'He thinks a lot of everyone,' Kestrel said. 'Like one of those dogs that'll follow any old gin home.'

'Ah, Kes, for Christ's sake,' Rock said. 'You're spitting away like a mother-cat. Come off it.'

He grinned then, with his bent mouth, and looked quite amiable for a moment. 'Okay, Rocky, as you say.'

'Byrnie's all right,' said Jack.

'Sure,' said Kestrel. 'Byrnie's a good bloke, in his own language.' He wiped down the bar with a grey rag, and thought about something amusing.

'I'd better go,' said the diviner, putting down his glass.

'Ah, not yet,' Rock said. But the diviner was determined, and began to move back; only Byrne, who had finished dealing with Horse, reached out and grabbed him by the leg. And he went down like a thrown ram, sprawled over Horse's chest.

'Ah Christ,' said Kestrel, leaning over the bar to look, but grinning all the same. 'Can't anyone take this halfwit off my hands?'

'Replay,' Byrne shouted. 'Come on.'

Hard as he tried, the diviner couldn't disguise the fact that he was angry. His blue eyes were electric with it. He looked at Byrne, who was waiting with his arm up, and laughing, like a very innocent devil. Then he crawled off Horse and lay down on his belly, facing his attacker.

'Ignore the silly bastard,' said Rock; who had seen the diviner's face, and was afraid that he meant to hurt Byrne—to break his wrist, perhaps.

'It's all right,' the diviner said, very quiet and tense. He put up his arm, and they engaged.

Meanwhile Rock stood over them, hawk-eyed.

It was, I've heard, the longest and most tedious encounter that ever took place in that bar; and it was watched in silence, lasting a quarter of an hour. The earnestness of the diviner infected them; infected Byrne, too, who began to resist as if he were fighting for his life. They grunted, they sweated; they moved through an angle of a hundred and eighty degrees in their efforts to find the most rewarding position. And for minutes at a time they stared into each other's faces with a peculiar, though apparently meaningless, fixity. In their view, evidently, it had become a Homeric struggle. Even the spectators were not quite bored by it.

At last Byrne began to weaken. Very slowly his arm was forced downward. Then it hurt him, and he bit his lip. The diviner watched him intently.

'Give in, Byrnie,' Rock said.

'Yair,' Byrne whispered. 'Okay, give in. Give in, give in.' His voice suddenly rose to a yelp. 'I give in. Mike. Mike.'

Then Rock prodded the diviner in the ribs with the toe of his boot. And he, almost reluctantly, it seemed, let Byrne go and stood up, brushing his dusty trousers.

'You don't want to hurt him, do you?' Rock said, as if he were not too sure.

'No,' said the diviner, panting a little. 'No. You all right, Byrnie?' And suddenly he was recognizable again, he was prepossessing.

'I'm okay,' Byrne muttered. He staggered to his feet, rubbing his wrist, then reached for a glass on the bar and emptied it. 'I'm drunk,' he complained. It was obvious enough.

'Have another drink,' Kestrel said to the diviner. 'The house owes you something.'

'No,' he said, 'thanks,' standing awkward and confused, in a general air of anticlimax. 'I was going then.'

'Don't go,' Byrne said, turning back to him. 'You don't want to go yet.'

'Yes, I do,' said the diviner patiently.

'I'll wrestle you,' Byrne was so kind as to offer.

'No, thanks,' said the diviner; and did begin to go away. But this time Byrne leaped on him.

It was soon over; a brief struggle, followed by a startling thunk. And there was the diviner alone, in the middle of the room, looking annoyed; and there was Byrne on the floor, with his head against the brass footrail of the bar, and the blood welling from a gash above one satanic eyebrow. Everyone was surprised.

'Oh hell,' said the diviner. 'I'm sorry.' He knelt beside Byrne and lifted his wounded head.

Byrne was alternately laughing and moaning. 'What'd you do that for?' he wanted to know. 'Mike, what'd you do that for? Mike.'

'Why did you jump on me?' the diviner countered. 'I'm sorry. But you shouldn't have done it.'

'You hurt me,' Byrne accused him, in self-pity. 'What'd you want to hurt me for, Mike?' He groaned.

'For the love of Jesus,' Kestrel prayed, 'someone put him to bed. Rocky, Jack, deal with him, will you.'

Byrne sat up and squinted around, with an air of martyrdom. 'Mike can do it,' he said. 'Mike's the bugger that hurt me.'

'You had it coming,' Kestrel said. 'By God you did.' He looked angry.

'I'll see him off,' said the diviner, dragging him to his feet and propping him against the bar. 'What about his head? He's bleeding.'

'We can fix it here,' Kestrel said. He opened a cupboard and took out a bottle of iodine and some prehistoric sticking plaster, which he gave to the diviner. 'Don't think you're the first bloke that ever did his block with Byrnie in this bar.'

'But I didn't——' the diviner started to say, before thinking better of it. Instead he opened the bottle, and stood poised with it.

'Put your head back, drongo,' Kestrel said to Byrne. 'And shut your flicking eyes. You should know the drill by now.'

The diviner poured some of the stuff on Byrne's upturned face, and watched with remote interest as a thin line of it flowed down the gaunt and cratered cheek. Then he cut a piece of plaster with his knife and strapped up the wound. Then he said: 'Got a handkerchief? Wipe your eye before you open it.'

Byrne did so. When he stood away from the bar, he lurched. The crack on the head had finished him off, apparently.

'Put me to bed,' he requested, indistinctly. 'Mike——'

'Okay,' said the charitable diviner, looking at Kestrel. 'Which way?'

Kestrel took a lamp from under the bar and lit it, and gave it to him with a nod towards the far door. 'Along the veranda,' he said. 'Last room.'

So the diviner hauled Byrne's arm over his shoulder, took the lamp in his free hand and said: 'Good night.'

'Goo' night,' said Byrne, amiably.

Locked together, they staggered away.

As they clumped down the veranda Byrne asked in an injured tone: 'What d'you want to hurt me for, Mike? What for?'

'All right, all right,' said the diviner. 'We've all heard you. Is this the room?'

It was. The diviner set down the lamp on a hard kitchen chair and hoisted Byrne on to the bed; where he lay unmoving, with his black eyes fixed on the diviner's face.

'Are you right now?' the diviner asked him.

He thought about it, and said: 'Got to take my boots off. Deborah goes crook.' So the diviner performed that small service.

'Okay now?'

71

'Don't go yet,' Byrne said, or pleaded. 'Sit down for a bit.'

The diviner seated himself rather gingerly on the bed, and let his flaking countenance be gazed upon.

'Ah, mate,' said Byrne at last, with a long sigh, and took the diviner's hand. He was thoroughly maudlin.

The diviner drew back involuntarily, but conquered the temptation in an instant and bent over Byrne with savage eyes. The yellow lamplight gave those eyes a greenish tinge, more sea-like than ever. 'What's the matter with you?' he demanded, softly, but with an angry insistence. 'Why are you like this?'

'I'm damned, Mike,' said Byrne, crying. 'I'm damned.' It was very curious. His father had been a Catholic; but that Byrne should have remembered anything of him was barely possible, one would have thought. 'Don't go yet.'

'I won't go,' said the diviner, with his fingers biting into Byrne's lean shoulders. 'Not till you drop this crap you're giving me. What's up?'

'You wouldn't know,' Byrne said, tragically.

'No,' the diviner agreed. 'Not without you telling me.'

'It doesn't matter. Doesn't matter, Mike.'

'It doesn't matter a cracker to me. But it does to you, plain enough.'

'I'm drunk,' Byrne said.

'I know you are.'

'I'll be right in the morning. I'll work for you. Up at the mine.'

'You're a good bloke,' said the diviner, rather grudgingly.

72

Then Byrne reached up with both arms and hugged him in a rib-cracking embrace. It was one of those funny, embarrassing, touching gestures to which some drunken men are prone, when the last barriers are down and they stand revealed, quite naked, in their loneliness. And the diviner bore it very well. But he asked, after a while: 'Can I go now?'

'Yair,' said Byrne, 'go now. I'll see you in the morning.'

So the diviner rose and went, with an uncertain expression about his mouth. And Byrne's dark face turned on the pillow to watch him, and his black eyes were fixed on the door long after he had disappeared.

FIVE

In the morning Charlie Yandana came and squatted outside my door; and as on that day I was feeling well-disposed, I went out and spoke to him. I asked what news he had. He thought for a while, and said that Byrnie was drunk and singing all last night.

I said I had heard him.

Charlie had an odd sympathy for Byrne. 'Byrnie went up the mine 's morning,' he informed me, as his next item of interest. 'New fella went with him. Gunna make something.'

There was a light, dustless breeze blowing, and the day was not unduly hot by Tourmaline standards. I decided that I would go and spy on them; for I was consumed with curiosity about the diviner's doings. So I fetched my hat and set out, across the flat stretches north of the road, for the falling masts and grey roof of the sad dead Sons of Tourmaline mine.

Ah, but it was not cool. I sweated, climbing among the chaotic slate of the hill. Heat rose from the rocks around me. I feared for my heart. And such desolation everywhere. The slope honeycombed with the shafts of fossickers, predecessors and inheritors of the mine; broken walls and collapsed sheds, chunks and sheets and cylinders of useless iron, half buried in the grey sand of the mullock hill, with whose sterility no mere desert can ever compare. Such ruin I could not well describe in a language that has not, as yet, lost hope.

The mine office faced me as I crossed the ridge. Very handsome it is, of the same pale stone as the gaol, brought here from miles away, in the time of prosperity. It has two high gables at either end, each pierced by a round window with slats of green-painted wood, and each with a bay window at ground level. The long section joining these is recessed, making the slate-paved veranda very wide in that part. The veranda surrounds the building on all four sides, and is garnished above with wrought-iron lacework. In ancient times it was shaded with pepper trees, but these are dead now, like all the trees of Tourmaline.

I walked up the veranda to the end where I knew they would be, in the high cool hall where Jack Speed, for a small fee, does the smelting. Only this part is ever used now. It was long ago, when I was a young man at Laceys, that Tourmaline died ('died in the night', as old-timers used to say) and no equipment worth moving was left behind. The rest of the building, apart from Jack's living quarters, is an echoing shell, undisturbed even by vermin.

They were standing side by side, a short way from the forge, with their backs to me, as I entered. They were very alike; I had to look carefully at their hair to distinguish them. The diviner was holding the rod in his outstretched palms, experimentally.

'Is it done?' I asked. And, turning to see who it was, they showed me their downcast faces. So I knew that something was wrong.

'It's done,' Byrne said, 'but it isn't what he wanted. I dunno.'

'It's all right,' the diviner said. 'It's fine.' But he obviously didn't think so.

It seemed to be a simple Y of heavy-gauge wire, the loop of the foot forged solid and a small hook at the junction. From this hook hung a small pill bottle, filled with red-brown water. It looked a very crude contraption to base such extravagant hopes on.

'It's okay,' the diviner said again. 'Thanks, Byrnie.' He held it delicately in his open palms, as if questioning it.

'Ah well,' said Byrne, with resignation, 'we'll see, anyway.' He turned back to the forge, on which a black billy was sitting, and threw in a handful of tea from the packet he was holding. Then he picked up the billy with a pair of tongs and rotated it. 'Come and have a cuppa with Jack,' he invited me, leading the way out and along the veranda. So I drifted after him. But the diviner stayed behind, examining his new rod with a look of gloom.

Jack's room contained a sagging iron bed, a table, two chairs, a couple of kerosene cases, and a fifty-year-old calendar with a photograph of a partly nude girl hiding among balloons. On the table were a few cracked cups, a spoon, a bottle of sugar, and a small cube of gold.

I picked it up; asking: 'Whose is this?'

'The old fella's,' Jack said. He was lying on the bed, limp with boredom. 'He don't want it.'

A strange man, Dave Speed. I asked after him.

'He's all right,' Jack said. 'Least, I reckon he is. Hasn't been in for a couple of months. Last time he brought the stuff for that.'

'He does well,' I said.

Jack scratched his head, indifferent. 'He knows where to find it.'

'Anyone with him now?'

'Old Jim. Jimmy Bogada. That's all.'

'What do they do for water?'

'There's a well,' Jack said. 'Old stock route well.' He laughed. 'You ought to see it. They pull up half a bucket of mud, give it a day to settle, and then skim off the water. About a cupful.'

I weighed the gold in my hand; so rich, so heavy. 'But he finds it.'

'He's an old hand,' Jack said. 'He don't need no water. If it's a dollying show he knows all about it.'

He spoke with a certain pride of this man he hardly knew.

Byrne poured out the thick black tea and shouted for the diviner. He came presently, still carrying the rod, which he laid on the table in front of him. Tasting the tea, he grimaced.

'It's lousy water,' Jack apologized. 'You get used to it.'

'He's not going to have to,' said Byrne.

The diviner gave a perfunctory smile.

'What do you plan for today?' I asked him. When one is old one tends to take this tone.

'I don't know,' he said. 'What is there?' And again he seemed to be going through one of his fits of inertia, which so profoundly depressed us all.

'Where have you been?' I asked, battling the listlessness. 'Have you seen the gaol? Or the church? Or the garden?'

'No,' he said; 'nothing like that.'

'Come with me, then—if you're not doing anything?'

'Now?' He pushed away his cup, languidly. 'All right, if you want to.'

'Have you got a hat?'

'Out there,' he said, going to get it. I rose too, picking up the rod, and thanking Jack for his hospitality.

'Come again,' he said, from where he lay sprawling. 'Bet you haven't been here for years.'

'No,' I began to say, 'not since——' Then I saw Byrne and Jack glance at one another, and caught back the reminiscence. Ah, but they hurt me, the young.

The diviner came back to the doorway, wearing his hat. We moved away together, down the broad-flagged veranda; which was once cool with shade and sharp with the smell of pepper trees, droning with bees through the brief month of spring.

'What a place to let go,' the diviner said, looking back as we picked our way through the flotsam of the mine.

I sighed. And we went on in silence, until the edge of the hill was reached, and Lake Tourmaline stretched out to the north of us like a flat pink desert. Towards the horizon it was flooded with mirage, very sky-blue, mirroring a few dead trees on the far shore.

'This is the lake,' I said. 'The bird life is interesting in a good season.'

He laughed, scanning the outlook. Far away to the east, by the lake edge, the remains of another and older mine were still visible. Before us, the roofs of a few very derelict tin shanties glared and shimmered.

'What's that?' he asked, pointing.

'The native camp,' I said. He nodded.

We went on down the hillside, picking our way between the disused shafts, some partly hidden with dead brushwood and sheets of old iron, others still keeping the forlorn remnants of shelters. On the flat ground between the two hills it was the same. But a proper track led up the easier gradient to the church. I was relieved, I confess, for my heart was beating heavily.

In front of the church stood the dark oleander, flowering in this season; and in front of the oleander, as we came up, an old coloured woman was squatting to urinate. When she heard our footsteps she sprang to her feet and vanished, instantly, like a bird.

The diviner burst out laughing. 'Who was that?'

'I think it was Gloria,' I said. 'Deborah's grandmother.' And I too began to laugh, until I felt quite helpless, and he looked at me strangely. 'I do believe,' I tried to explain to him, 'she's been keeping that tree alive all these years.'

We stood on the beaten earth before the church, looking up. The stone cross rose sharp and pale against the sky. Sheets of iron had fallen from the roof; the glass was missing from most of the narrow windows, the wooden bell tower, a little removed from the door, was far gone in ruin. But it was beautiful: especially beautiful in the smell of flowers. I stood inhaling the fragrance of the oleander, wondering whether this scent was known to Byrne, to Jack, to Kestrel.

The diviner pushed the cracked door, which shuddered and scraped across the floor as it retreated. He took off his hat. We went into the cool place, half shadow, half sunlight, roofed in part by the sky. The pews were there still. It was very bare. It was also very clean. I was surprised.

And on the altar, which stood, at that time of day, in the light—on the altar there were oleander flowers in a tin mug, brilliantly glowing. And ranged about them were pieces of packing-case wood, on which someone had written in charcoal: MARY MOTHER OF GOD; GOD THE FATHER; JESUS LOVER OF MANKIND; FATHER SON AND HOLY GHOST. And also: GOD SAVE OUR QUEEN. I stood amazed.

'It must be the old woman,' the diviner said, very hollowly in that empty place. And he stood staring, reverent.

'The queen of heaven, I suppose,' I said at last, for the sake of speaking. He did not respond. I tried to remember something of Gloria—but what was there to know? A nondescript old woman, whose name I would never have noted if she had not been Agnes Day's mother.

And he was very serious about it: so serious that he moved aside to a pew, and knelt, to my great astonishment, and I suppose said a prayer. I cannot tell why this harmless gesture impressed me so uncomfortably; but I found that I could not stay there with him, and so went out again to stand beside Gloria's tree, inhaling its heavy sweetness as I looked over Tourmaline.

80

He joined me presently, saying nothing. But he took his knife and cut off a branch of oleander, and trimmed this into two short lengths, which he forced onto the ends of his rod as handgrips. And again he affected me unpleasantly, in a way I cannot define. There was something too easy, uncalled for, in this pious act. I made no remark on it.

When he had done paring the sticks, which cannot have been very suitable for his purpose, he came over to stand beside me and look at the town. I pointed out my gaol, which he had not seen before, and the dusty greenish square of Rock's vegetable garden, surrounded by an iron fence to keep off the searing winds. Beyond, pale shapes were moving.

'The goats,' I said, as he pointed. 'There's a trough there. But we can't keep many. There isn't the water.'

He asked, idly, if there were wild goats; but agreed immediately afterwards that it was a foolish question. All the while his eyes were moving up and down the township, and the rod quivered in his thin hands.

'Where will I live?' he asked at length.

'You can choose,' I said, waving my hand at the prospect. 'It's all yours.'

'Where's Byrnie's place?'

I pointed along the hillside. He looked, but only with difficulty distinguished the three miners' huts I meant him to see: mere boxes of piled-up stone, daubed here and there with mud, and roofed with loose sheets of iron weighed down by boulders.

'It's not much,' he said.

'He hasn't got much—poor Byrnie.'

'Who else lives there?'

'Only Byrnie. The other two are empty.'

'I'll go there,' he said; and stood meditating.

'You haven't got much in the way of money,' I began to say; hesitantly, because I was not sure how he would take it. And he looked round sharply.

'Oh,' he said, 'you know that.'

'But everyone will help you out. Let them. We need you, badly.'

'I'll go in with Jack and Byrnie,' he said. 'I'll go prospecting.' And he went on, in a quick shy mumble: 'I've got a—a gift, in that line,' as I remembered having heard him say before.

He brooded over the town. 'Who wants money, anyway? Who wants it here? Or gold, rather.'

'There's the truck,' I reminded him. 'We're not self-sufficient.'

'Why can't we be?' he demanded. 'Get rid of the grog, and so on. A—a Utopia we could have, with the water.'

'With the water,' I echoed, glancing at his profile as he gazed out over Tourmaline. The nostrils of his fine straight nose were dilated, his mouth was tense. A sullen blue light smouldered in his eyes, under the fair lashes. I did not know what to think of him.

'I could save this place,' he said—so quietly and matter-of-factly that the queerness of this claim did not hit me for a moment. When it did, I began to fear him.

'From what?' I said. 'Save it from what?'

But he turned away, with a sigh, swinging the rod in one hand, and picked off a flower from the bush, and held it to his nostrils. 'It doesn't matter,' he said, after a while;

quite carelessly, as if I had tediously interrupted something. 'Just thinking aloud.'

'I can't understand you,' I said.

He gave a wry smile; not for my benefit.

'You can save it with water. Is that what you meant?'

'Yes,' he said. 'That's it.' And turning back from surveying the church he suggested that I might care to go home.

He came with me down the hill, and I invited him to inspect my gaol. The papers in the yard seemed to interest him. Digging about with his foot, he asked whether I might have such a thing as an old survey map of the area. But I could not remember anything of that kind, and he looked displeased. He seemed about to ask me how such masses of paper came to be in the yard; and I was glad when he stopped, as I could not have explained to a stranger, and one so young, the despair that had driven me to this gesture, after years and years of hopeless waiting. He would not, I judged, understand the anguish of old men.

Later I took him to the garden, which was then at its worst. Rock was not there. The diviner looked about him with a slightly contemptuous air, which I found it difficult to pardon, although he was evidently unconscious of it. We both refrained from any mention of water.

He returned with me to my house for a wretched meal which I prepared in a few minutes. The house seemed to intrigue him. He poked around for a time among my few books, pored over the wall map, and glanced repeatedly at the wireless, with an enigmatic smile. I did not know what to make of him. After a whole morning in his company

I was beginning to find him in many ways oppressive; so very remote, at times not altogether human. And yet, at other times, especially when he laughed, I could see nothing in him but a charming and candid boy, to whom my soft old heart warmed in an instant. He was confusing. I could not fathom him.

When he had eaten, he said he would go up the hill again, to look at the empty huts, and took his leave of me. I stood at my back door and watched him. The lean blue figure slowly climbed the path, turned a bend and was gone. And above, on the hilltop, church and skeletal bell tower loomed flat and sharp, as if drawn with a fine pen on the sky.

Suddenly he too was there, a dark moving line. He paused for a moment to look down on Tourmaline. I saw his arm go up as he shaded his eyes. Then he merged into the church wall, and vanished.

That same day he told Tom and Mary that he would leave them in the morning to take up his quarters in one of the stone huts. Mary was unwilling to let him go; but he insisted, with that cool stubbornness of his, that they had done enough for him already. He did, however, accept a bed and some cooking gear, to be carried up to the hut later by Charlie Yandana and his brother, besides a little food which Mary forced on him.

'You must come down and see us,' she instructed him. 'Often. Especially when those black dogs get on your back. We don't want you to be lonely.'

'The black dogs are gone,' he said; promising, offhand,

to come there now and again. Then he picked up his blanket and a billy or two, and went off past the gaol to his new home.

When Deborah saw him go, she began to think of things she might have done for him. 'I'll take him some dinner,' she said, 'already cooked.'

'He's not paralysed, is he?' asked Kestrel. 'I never saw you running round with tucker for Jack or Horse.'

'Jack and Horse are always here,' she said.

'Ah, leave him alone, poor bastard. He won't want women clucking round him when he's just got away from Mary.'

She looked at him, frigidly, and went ahead with her intention. And in the afternoon she went trailing up the hill to his hut, a billy in her hand.

Those square flat-roofed humpies are deceptive. The room inside is larger than one would suppose, and higher too, for the floor, of bare earth, is sunken a foot or two below the surrounding level. There is a doorway (doorless) and a window-place (windowless) and a good deal of air and light flowing in through the innumerable crannies of the walls. At one end is a fireplace, rather neatly made, even handsome, in which the diviner had rigged up a tripod for his cooking. Two tins of water stood nearby, and there were dishes and things stacked on a packing case. The bed had also arrived. It was on this that the diviner was sitting, deep in some book of Tom's he had brought with him.

He looked up sharply as the dark shape of her loomed in the doorway. The light, coloured by floor and walls, turned the skins of both of them very red, and made his

85

eyes rather pale and startling. It was hot under the flat roof. His upper lip was gleaming.

'It's you,' he said. 'I couldn't think——' And he stood up, courteously; though she had the impression, not for the first time, that he was ill at ease and not pleased to see her.

'I've brought you some food,' she said, stepping down into the room. 'Because it's your first day here, and we don't know what kind of a cook you are.'

He made an awkward gesture. 'You shouldn't do that. I'm used to looking after myself.'

'Oh well,' she said, 'it's no trouble.'

Looking about him, in his confused way, he asked: 'Should I light the fire?'

'No, it's still hot. I've been walking in the sun. This is a warm house you've picked.'

'Yes,' he agreed, vaguely; and as an afterthought invited her to sit down.

She perched herself on the edge of the bed, which had nothing on it but a grey blanket with a broad blue stripe, and quietly watched him. He was definitely uneasy, swinging the billy in his lean hand. 'I suppose,' he said at last, 'you've eaten already?' She nodded. 'Oh well, then——' He pulled off the lid, and a cloud of steam rose.

'You don't mind if I watch you,' she said, 'do you? It's hot walking.'

'No,' he said, 'no, don't go yet,' pouring out the stew, of salted goat meat, into a plate, and reaching for a spoon. He mumbled disjointedly as he ate, still standing. 'This is very good. Sorry about the heat. Don't know why everyone has to do so much for me.'

'You're a stranger,' she said. 'And a diviner as well.'
And all the time the unmannerly girl stared at him.

He caught her at it, and looked quickly down. 'You
don't get many strangers, I reckon.'

'Not a one,' said Deborah. 'You know that.'

'Sure, I do,' he admitted. 'I'm just talking.'

Then out of the blue, while he was lifting a spoonful
to his mouth, she said to him: 'You aren't happy, are you?'

The spoon hung suspended, and he looked at her.
'What makes you say that?'

'I can tell. Do you want to go away again?'

'My oath, I don't.'

'Sometimes I'd like to go,' she said, avoiding his eyes
now, and craning her neck a little to look out of the window.
'Just for a while.'

'You'd never come back.'

'That's what they all say.'

'You've talked about it, have you? To your husband?'

'No,' she said, 'I couldn't tell Kes that. He's not easy
to talk to.'

His eyes kept returning. She wore one of her several
blue dresses, which the small sharp breasts strained against,
and her thick hair was loosely tied behind. She was very
slender and long-waisted. Her eyes were deep, and with
a certain sombreness, even when she smiled, showing
between the full lips her perfect teeth, like chips of quartz.
She was rather fine. Only her legs were imperfect, a little
too lean; and her feet, from having gone barefoot all her
life, were on the broad side.

'How old are you?' he asked, putting down his plate.

'Eighteen,' she said.

'As young as that——'

'I'm old,' she said. 'I feel it. I don't know.'

'And you reckoned *I* wasn't happy.'

'I'm happy enough,' she said, swinging her long bare legs, 'if that's what you mean. Only——'

'Only what?' he asked, guardedly.

'I don't know,' she sighed. And then: 'Have you ever,' watching him, 'been in love?'

His mouth went hard. He resented the atrocious liberty.

'No,' she said, 'please. Don't be wild with me. You're young too. I want to know.'

'Why?' he asked, in a dampening tone.

'Because——I don't know. I mean, I don't know if—what it's like.'

'Maybe I don't either.'

'You must.'

He pushed some crockery aside and sat down on the packing case, with his arms folded around his blue knees and his eyes on the floor. 'I don't know what you're talking about,' he said after a time. He was not even courteous any longer.

'I'm coloured,' she said. 'P'r'aps I expect too much for a coloured woman.'

'Ah, bull,' said the diviner.

'People can think they love anything. Anything at all. Just whatever's there.'

'You could be right.'

'They have to love. It doesn't matter about being loved—not at first. Loving's the main thing.'

88

He shifted on his packing case, still earnestly examining the ground between his boots. 'Where does this get us?'

'In the end?'

'In the end.'

She laughed. She looked quite gay. 'How would I know? I told you, I'm eighteen.'

He shook his head, slow and brooding.

'I'll tell you,' she said, leaning forward. 'It starts with loving anything, whatever's there. And it finishes with wanting to be loved back. And you could be unlucky.'

'I don't reckon,' he said, in a low voice, 'you should tell these things all over Tourmaline.'

'But I don't. Only to you.'

'The other day, at Tom's place——'

'Only to you,' she repeated.

'Oh hell,' he protested, standing up, 'I'm not—I'm not—I don't get this at all.'

'You're wild with me,' she gently accused him.

'No, I'm not. I'm grateful. It was bloody good of you to bring me up that tucker. But for God's sake——'

'You swear too much,' she said. And that stopped him in his tracks like barbed wire. He sat down again.

'I don't mean it,' she said.

'Didn't mean what?'

'Anything. I was trying to joke with you.'

'Ah, well,' he said, with a cornered look, 'sorry if I sound dumb.'

'You're nice to talk to.'

'Nice of you to say it,' he replied, rather sullen in his insincerity.

'I'll take the billy home now, if you've finished.'

'Good,' he said, rising to fetch it. 'And thanks again.'

'Can I come another time?'

'It's a hot walk,' he hedged. 'And I'll see you in the pub, sometimes.'

'It's different. Kes doesn't like you.'

He stopped in his movement. 'Is that so?' he said, after a moment. 'He doesn't show me that.'

'He doesn't show things.'

'Why would he feel that way?'

'He's jealous,' she said simply. 'He's not a diviner. And no one likes him much, except Byrnie.'

'And you.'

She shrugged. 'It's different,' she said again.

So he said no more, but held out the billy to her. And she slid her brown legs to the floor, and stood up, and reached for it.

'Well, goodbye,' he said.

'Goodbye,' said Deborah, graciously. And with those slender flanks stirring under the blue dress (a beautiful gait she had; he must have noticed, looking after her) she took herself out of the doorway and down the slope.

He lay down on the bed and stared up at the iron roof, at the rough crossbeams with the bark still on them. I am imagining, of course; I am imagining him as I so often saw him later when I went to the hut. But what he looked like when he was alone, and what he thought—these things I will not imagine. He was too confusing. I will not try to pin him down.

Deborah, meanwhile, went down the hill to the road,

and down the road to the hotel, and quietly into the kitchen. But Kestrel heard her, and called out: 'How was the witch-doctor?'

'Ha ha ha,' she sneered, as she bashed the billy. 'Very funny, Reginald.' For that was his unexpected name.

SIX

It was a rare month that brought Dave Speed to Tourmaline. That was why, when I saw him trudging up the road late one morning, apathetically followed by old Jimmy Bogada, I came quickly from my house and called after him.

He turned and walked back, pushing the greasy hat from his forehead. A peculiar lop-sided gait he had, like a drunken stockman.

'Long time since you've been here,' I said.

'Had no reason,' said Dave, in his furry meandering voice, as he put down the bag that was slung over his shoulder and wiped his forehead. 'How's things with you?'

I was fine, I said. And he?

'Not so bad,' said Dave. 'Getting old, but.'

To me, I said, he seemed a young fella still.

'Time flies,' he said. 'And who'd want to stop it if they could?'

He was the thinnest man I ever saw, not much more than a skeleton in his ragged clothes, and he did not look strong. For years he had seemed to be an alcoholic. Then, suddenly, in the space of a day or two, he was one no longer. But he never lost the mannerisms. Even now, one would have guessed from his slurred speech and rolling walk that he was half-seas-over. He was blind in one eye, too, and I may say in all charity that he looked a ruin. Yet something about him, in spite of everything, drew one's attention, like a bird in the Tourmaline sky.

'You're going to see Jack,' I supposed.

'Might as well,' he said, offhand. 'Got some stuff for him.' He was always in two minds about Jack, whom he had almost ignored when he was a boy. He had been heard to say that he reckoned the young one was a better man than his father; but he had said it with a trace of resentment in his pleasure.

'He's okay, is he?' he asked. 'The young bloke? Ah, sure, he always is. Wish I'd had his sense when I was his age.'

'You enjoyed yourself,' I consoled him.

'You reckon?' He gave his sudden sharp drunken laugh.

'I hear you do well out there, at that show of yours.'

'We do okay,' he said, 'Jimmy and me. It's a healthy life.'

And I had a sudden vision of his camp; the old stock route well in its platform of stones, the antique winch and bucket, the humpy (supposing they had one) of dead grey brushwood. And the flat bare blood-red country radiating out to the horizons, aglare with broken quartz.

'You're a lucky man,' I brought myself to say. But what

did they eat, I wondered? Tea and damper, probably, and the odd tin of meat as a luxury. He was as much a native as Jimmy Bogada, and had learned the same tolerance of deprivation.

'Better go to Tom's,' he said. 'See about some stores.' And I almost laughed to think what fare they were going to carry back that day, to their larder ten miles away. 'See you later.'

He turned and went; and old Jimmy, who had been squatting by the roadside, fell in behind him without a word. I could not help smiling as I watched them, they had such curious and contrasting ways of walking; Dave rolling like a sailor, and Jimmy (very straight for an old man) stalking behind with all the stealthy purpose of a black hunter. And they had come in to go shopping. It sounded almost suburban.

When they came to the store Jimmy broke ranks, as it were, and went to sit under the veranda, while Dave went in to see Tom. And he was so featureless, old Jimmy, so much a part of any landscape whatsoever, that I doubt whether anyone (supposing anyone had passed) would have remarked to himself: 'Jimmy Bogada', or looked about for Dave. He simply was; a dark human shape, wriggling its toes in the velvety dust.

In the store, Tom came out of his usual trance, or open-eyed sleep, and smiled. 'You, Dave.'

'How's the man?' said Dave. 'Looking fit.'

'So are you. Out of tucker?'

'Yair, sort of. Give us the usual, when you get time, and dump it by the door there. We'll pick it up in the morning.'

'Stay the night with us?'

'Ah, she's right,' Dave said. 'Thanks all the same. I'll be going up the mine. Reckon it won't hurt the young bloke to do his old man a favour.'

'Still getting rich?'

'To hell with that,' said Dave. 'It's a hobby.'

'You're right,' Tom said. 'You can't spend it. Give it to Jack.'

'What's he going to do with it? He's no booze artist— or is he?'

'Not much.'

'Which way do you mean "not much"?'

'He doesn't drink much. Relax.'

'Ah,' said Dave. 'Well, fair enough. Because I'd kick his arse for him if he did, big as he is.'

'Old Puritan you turned out to be,' Tom said.

Dave gave his drunken laugh. Then he laid himself out on the counter, propped at one elbow, and looked amicably at Tom.

'Well, what's the news?' he wanted to know. 'Young Deborah still with Kes?'

''Fraid so.'

'That's no good. Jack should have got her. Anything out of the camp'd do for Kes.'

'Kes might say the same for Jack,' said Tom.

'Ah, he's a gin-jockey too, is he? Young bastard.'

'Man's an animal,' said Tom. 'Don't get too virtuous.'

'You get worked,' said Dave in a friendly tone. And he went on, pondering: 'Funny thing. Old Jim tells me there's hardly been a kid born in the camp for years. What do you make of that?'

'Despair,' said Tom, moving his thin shoulders. 'I heard somewhere about how they were dying out in the old days, just the same. It was the change, the white men coming. The blokes reckoned they couldn't find the spirits of the children. So they stopped breeding.'

'Ah,' said Dave, 'not enough jigjig.'

'That's what some missionary told them. And did they laugh. No, it's one of those mind over matter things—you know?'

'She's a weird old world,' Dave decided, after giving the matter due thought. 'I can't make her out at all.'

'Keep trying,' Tom said. 'I've got a lot of faith in your opinions, Dave.' He grinned at him, defended in irony. 'I reckon you must get some thinking done out there.'

'Don't come that on me,' said Dave. 'It's not the time, it's having the stuff to think with.' He shifted his knobbly hip on the hard counter, grunting. 'You've told me bugger-all so far. What's been happening?'

'There's only one bit of news you're likely to hear anywhere,' Tom said. 'About the diviner.'

'Who's that?' asked Dave. He was slightly deaf. 'Not the Law,' he supposed (and Tom told me later), 'gone and made himself archbishop?'

'Diviner,' Tom said. 'Dowser. He says he's going to find water for us.' And he went on to give Dave a short history of our new citizen, from the time that the driver stepped out of the truck and announced his unprecedented find.

Dave listened poker-faced. When Tom had done, he breathed out a sort of sigh.

'It's the end,' he said.

'You're a queer coot. Everyone else says it's the beginning.'

'You too?'

'I don't know. Yes, I do too. We like water, don't we?'

'Sure we like it,' Dave said. 'But do we like strangers blowing in and sending the word round they got special powers to change the place?'

'He never said that. We wouldn't know he was a diviner if the Law hadn't dragged it out of him while he was sick.'

'He's a fake,' Dave said.

'I don't think he is,' said Tom. 'Or if he is, he doesn't know it.'

'What's he like? Big talker?'

'Not a bit of it. Quiet. But not,' Tom added after a moment, 'not still. Know what I mean?'

'Sounds like Kes.'

'You're right,' Tom said. 'Funny. Hadn't thought of it.'

'Kes in favour of him?'

'No. He's the only one.'

'It's the end,' Dave said again.

'You want us all to go native,' Tom said. 'That's what you've got against him. Just enough food and water to keep us alive and no distractions. Dave Speed's Utopia.'

'And what's wrong with it?' Dave demanded. 'I know what I'm talking about. All the years I spent when I was the town drunk, wanting to be a tree.'

'Seems to me you've got there.'

'So now I want to be a stone. And I'll get there too.'

'Won't we all?' Tom said. 'It's death you mean.'

'Maybe,' said Dave. 'Well, you can't get much quieter than that.'

He swung his legs to the floor and stood up. 'Better go and see young Jack. Be back in the morning.'

'Good to see you again,' Tom said, meaning it. 'I'll tell Mary to have some breakfast for you.'

'I can see Jack's going to bash my ear about this divining.'

'Sure to. It's the talk of the town. And you might come round.'

'I might,' said Dave, standing there with his hands in his pockets, and his one good eye, of a light clear grey, on Tom. 'There's no getting away from it, the idea of water is pretty strong. You and me can remember when that pub veranda was covered all round with passion-vines, and bloody good it was, too, to sit out there at this time of day, with a schooner, in the cool. And what the Law remembers I wouldn't like to ask him, because I'd never get away if he started to tell. But the place is better now than it ever was then. We've got to the bare bones of the country, and I reckon we're getting to the bones of ourselves. If the water comes, it'll be when we've stopped needing it. We're coming true, mate.'

'You're a blackfellow,' Tom said; 'or one of these desert saints.'

'I'm a drongo,' said Dave. 'I'm a kid. I don't know anything. They say the grass is greener on the other side of the fence. Well, when I was in the grass I liked the look of the desert. And now I'm in the desert I like it even better.'

'And not a flower around,' said Tom. 'Not a roo, not a cocky, not a bee.'

'The human race is the toughest thing going,' Dave

said. 'And the greediest, and the dumbest. Maybe I don't understand this joker. But we wouldn't want an emperor of Tourmaline.'

He stooped as he spoke, picking up his bag from the floor, and went out with a wooden face to rouse Jimmy Bogada.

That night, at the mine, in the small yellow circle of a hurricane lantern islanded in the obscurity of Jack's tall room, Dave put forward his views once again; to the annoyance of his son, and the polite disbelief of Rock, their visitor. He was a hopeless case, Jack suggested; a born pessimist, a true old-timer who wanted to keep even the worst things exactly as he was used to knowing them. And anyway, did he think Tourmaline had always been like this? He was raving, said Jack.

He knew what he was talking about, said Dave. He had lived a bit longer than either of them, as they bloody well knew, and he didn't need any young fella of twenty-five to straighten his ideas out for him. The trouble with Tourmaline was that too many people listened to the Law, whose memory wasn't worth *that* much (snapping, naturally, his fingers) nowadays, and who had always been given to queer notions, as anyone of Dave's age could confirm.

Rock said quietly that he thought the Law, for all his faults, had a fair recollection of things as they had been; but that was not the argument. The point was whether they wanted water or not; and could there be any doubt that they did? In which case the diviner, if anyone, was the man to find it.

Dave repeated his arguments, in a louder voice, and with a new and (as it were) religious conviction. He seemed to preach complete passivity to the drought, to the desert, to the sun. This view Jack rejected with scorn. Dave then demanded to know where the diviner lived, and said he would set out instantly to interview him and make a reliable assessment of the man. But he was talked out of this, on the grounds of the darkness outside and the many abandoned shafts between the mine and the diviner's hut. At last Rock went home, and father and son went to bed, still arguing. And as things happened, Dave had lost interest by the time he woke in the morning. So he did not meet the diviner, and was not able to give us his reliable and informed opinion of that most controversial figure in Tourmaline's history.

At the same time as this debate was going on, Tom and Mary were sitting in their kitchen, where they had a habit of passing the evenings, when Deborah suddenly appeared in the doorway, panting, and looking wild.

Mary got up and went to her, without a word. She put her arms about her. And the tall girl bent her head to Mary's soft neck and wept a little.

'I hate him,' she announced, when this was over.

Mary patted her shoulder, murmuring something.

'Come home, Deb,' Tom said. He pulled up a chair for her at the kitchen table, to which Mary led her. And they sat down together, the three of them, and looked at each other, their chins on their hands.

'There's no need for you to stay with him,' Mary said, after a time.

'No,' said Deborah. 'I won't. I won't. I think he hates me.'

'He's got a bitter tongue,' Tom said. 'But he doesn't mean all he says, maybe.'

'He's cruel to me,' she raged, still reliving whatever quarrel it was that had driven her out of the hotel. 'He's so insulting. And he hates Michael. He says I love Michael. He must be mad.'

Perfectly mild in the contemplation of her fury, Tom asked whether she would stay the night.

'I'll stay for always,' she swore.

'You know you won't. You'll go back to him in the morning.'

'No, Pa! Not ever.' She appealed to Mary. 'You believe me, don't you?'

'I don't know,' Mary said. 'You're always changing your mind about him.'

'He's always changing,' she said. 'Not me. Sometimes he's so—— Sometimes I love him, I do really. And then he gets like he is tonight. He wants to own me, like a dog. The way he owns poor Byrnie. I can't stay with him.'

'And you want to own him, too,' Tom pointed out. 'And he won't stand for that. The trouble is, you're both in love. It's not comfortable.'

She lifted her dark hand to her forehead, and sat staring at the tabletop, quite wretched.

'Will you go to bed now?' Mary asked, soothingly.

'I'm so tired,' Deborah said. 'He makes me so tired.' And she did look it, with her neck wearily bent, and the lamplight on the crests of the waves in her brown hair.

'I'll never go back,' she promised again. But Tom was right to look at Mary with a faint smile. Because she was gone in the morning, she was in the hotel again, moodily cooking breakfast for her man; with one of those flourbag handkerchiefs she sometimes dabbed at her scowling brow.

SEVEN

So now I come to what may be the most important of the events I did not actually see; and again I must imagine and invent, I must place in a framework the bare narratives given me by Byrne and the diviner.

The diviner had told me at the church that he would turn to prospecting before long, that he would work in with Byrne or Jack Speed; but I had not paid much attention. I thought that water was his first object. After that, of course, I assumed, with all the others, that the whole town would return to the gold, and that everyone, the diviner included, would grow rich. But he thought otherwise. He meant, as it turned out, to grow, or to make us, rich first.

And one day, with this in mind, he called for Byrne and suggested that they walk out to Byrne's claim; a paltry affair on a hillock four miles from Tourmaline. I saw them go, glancing out of my door by chance. The diviner carried his rod in one swinging hand. Byrne trailed behind him with a waterbag, looking very much like old Jimmy Bogada.

They walked for a little over an hour through the hard red stony desert (it is a desert now, I may call it that) with Byrne's hillock like a mountain in front of them, visible all the way, rising out of a flatness so absolute that one can see the curve of the world at the horizons. And when they got there, sweating rather heavily even in that bone-dry air, the diviner was ill again, racked with one of his recurring headaches. So he wet his hair from the waterbag and lay down in the shade of a small open cave where Byrne kept his tools; for he camped there occasionally. And Byrne occupied himself in the meantime by knapping and dollying what he picked out as a 'kindly stone'.

He had no luck with that, however, and before he could begin another the diviner was on his feet again, pushing back his dank hair and replacing his hat. From his pocket he took a little knob of gold, and put it into the bottle that hung from his rod. Then he walked down to the foot of the hill. Byrne ambled after him, at a distance.

He looked quite absorbed, so Byrne told me later, standing there, with the rod between his hands. He held it with his palms up, forcing the forks slightly apart, and his eyes were fixed on the end of it. Frowning, very tense, he seemed to be entering a sort of trance; and he inspired such awe in his talkative friend, as he stood watching, that not one question escaped him. Throughout the progress of the ritual Byrne followed in a doglike silence.

With his stiff neck bent a little, the diviner stepped out, and began to follow around the foot of the hill; very slow in his movements, and still concentrating profoundly on the tip of the rod. These proceedings occupied ten minutes or more. Then he stopped dead in his tracks, quite rigid, and looking (said Byrne) as if he were listening to something. The rod was still steady and level.

He turned left and went on, away from the hillock, out towards the stone-littered plain. And Byrne, trailing behind, saw the rod straining in his hands. Suddenly it had defeated him, and was pointing downwards—straight downwards. And the handgrips of ecclesiastical oleander had disintegrated in his hands. He took another step, and stopped. The rod fell to the ground. He looked up, exhausted.

'There's a reef,' he said, very quiet and weary. 'Few feet of overburden. Old-timers missed it. Mark it, will you.'

Then he picked up the rod and went up the slope again to the rock-shelter. And there he lay down and went to sleep.

Byrne, in the meantime, in a haze of doubt and excitement, made a pile of stones on the spot where the diviner had stood and went to fetch his pick and shovel. Having almost no water he could not be subtle about testing the surface for gold. He simply dug.

And the reef was there. The cap of the reef was there.

With a great shout he bounded up the hill to the diviner.

In my terrible loneliness I grow elegiac. The news of this find, so great for Tourmaline, in which the diviner promised that all who cared to work it might have a share—this news left me less elated than melancholy. For I remembered how once it would have been received, with what rejoicings in the bar and pilgrimages over the countryside (not quite treeless, at that time) to the site of the discovery, with what prognostications of further greatness for Tourmaline. That was in the days of hope, in the days of tree-lined streets, the days when the verandas of the hotel and other buildings were shaded with vines, and oranges grew in what is now Rock's garden. Though they mock me for it, how can I forget? The glow of oranges in shining leaves, passion-fruit and -flower; the reds of oleander and bougainvillaea, the pepper trees' green-white drizzling flowers, sharp-smelling and loud with bees. These were the things I remembered, in my loneliness, when the news came of the diviner's find.

The town was moved, certainly, even excited. But gold means little now. It was the method of its tracking down that was the talk everywhere, the cause of all rumours and arguments. It was of water, not gold, that all thought after this miracle.

'What do you say now?' Byrne asked Kestrel. He was in the bar, but quite sober. 'Can he divine, or can't he?'

'I say he's a bloody good prospector,' said Kestrel; 'and the best bullduster I'm likely to meet.'

'You're so mean and jealous,' Deborah hissed at him. 'It's horrible.'

He turned on her, for a second, a bitter parody of a smile.

Tom Spring would say nothing. Divining, he confessed, he did not understand. He sat behind his counter like a small ivory statue of a sage, smiling luminously at Jack Speed, who brought the news.

'Don't you care?' Jack asked, incredulous. 'If he's as good as that, what about the water?'

'The water,' Tom mused. 'The water. I'm waiting, sure enough.'

'You sound like my old man.'

'I'm not,' Tom said. 'I believe in the boy—for some things. But the water: I'll wait and see about that.'

Rock brought me the tidings, his deepset brown eyes very bright and hopeful. He too thought less of the gold than of the augury.

'Kes is right to call him the witch-doctor,' he considered. 'Not natural, somehow.'

'He told us he had a gift,' I said. 'It looks as if he has.'

'I'm scared,' said Rock. 'Scared to hope too much.' And he looked across the road at the iron fence of his garden. 'Are we going to get this water? If we are, how long's it going to be?'

'How long?' I echoed, looking about me in a sort of trance; seeing trees spring up and flowers in the street, hearing sounds of sheep and birds in the far green distance. Why, in my great hope, did I remember the easter lilies in our old garden; the smooth pink lilies, so tough, so delicate, that sprang up leafless from the baked ground, before the earliest rains?

And the diviner, all this time, was in the church. What did he do there? I cannot truly say, for only one person ever saw him. That was old Gloria, self-appointed vergeress, who perhaps at that very moment was engaged in watching him. He was kneeling, she told me, before the altar, his head bowed, in a patch of sunlight. And I can see him, clearly enough, in the raw blue of his new clothes; his red young neck encroached upon by golden down, red dust on his boots and at the hip-pockets of his trousers. And his hair burning bright, like chaff in a thread of sunlight, such as may steal in through a nail-hole in a shed roof; and did, long ago, at home.

I imagine him striving, striving to empty his mind, as Tom seemed dedicated to do, awaiting some infusion of force and wisdom. I imagine him. That is all. Ah, but how difficult it is to re-create this young man, who to everyone meant something, and to no two people the same. Can I trust the testimony of Gloria Day, who also knelt before the altar, and was the only one to do so, if he did not? He remains obscure, confusing. I cannot pin him down.

He was there, at any rate, when she came in. And he heard her, and came quickly before she could escape.

'Here you are,' he said. 'I've been waiting for you. For days.'

The old dark woman, with her hair tied in a gaping rag, only looked at him. Glowing, mistrustful eyes she had.

'How long have you been coming here?' he asked her. 'Cleaning the place, and writing' (he pointed at the altar) 'these?'

She stood with her hands clasped across her stomach, searching him.

'Don't be scared,' he said. 'How many years?'

'Ah, long time,' she said at last, unwillingly, in her rather rich and deep voice. 'When the roof was on I start coming.'

'Why?' he gently asked.

'For God,' she said, quite simply.

'You love God?'

'Yes.'

'Do you know why?'

She never moved or looked away from him. 'God very big,' she said.

'Very big.'

'I want him to come.'

'Here?'

'Here. I keep this house clean for him. Might be he come some day. I keep asking him.'

'And what if he comes?'

'Water,' she said. 'Kangaroo, duck, everything. People pretty hungry in the camp now.'

'What do you ask him?'

'I ask him to make it rain,' she said. 'And the stones, I give him.' She pointed at the altar, where two round black pebbles, unnaturally smooth, lay before the wilted oleander flowers. 'Rain stones,' she said. 'He can make rain if he want to.'

'And no one else comes here to ask him that?'

'Only me. I come. No one else love God now. They all forget.'

'Everyone? Everyone forgets?'

'I think might be old Dave Speed and Jimmy Bogada love God too. But they don't live here. They don't care about his house.'

'Tom Spring, too? Mary Spring? Don't they love God?'

'I dunno,' she said. 'No one love his house. Only me.'

They stood gazing. She was in the shade, he in the sunlight. A rectangle of sky was above him. Over her shoulder, through the open door, the flowering oleander burned in the sun.

'You love God?' she asked, after a time.

'Yair,' he said. 'Yair.' His eyes were brilliant. He was looking into the light of the doorway. 'I love God, now. He's saved me.'

'Always?' she questioned. 'Always you love him?'

'No, not always. How was I to know?'

'He save you, all the same?'

'Against my will, maybe. Yair. He sent me to Tourmaline.'

'You still young,' she said.

'D'you know who I am?'

''Course. You the diviner.'

'D'you believe I've found God?'

'I dunno,' she said. 'How you tell?'

'Through pain,' he said—half-laughing, she told me, in a very strange way. 'Shame. Weakness. He makes me suffer. Persecutes me. Won't let me go. So I know I've found him.'

He lifted his hand to push back his flopping forelock. His hand was shaking.

'You don't hate God?' she asked, uncertain.

'No, no, I love him. Have to. There's nothing else.'

'Nothing else,' she repeated. 'Only God. Nothing else.'

'Pray for me.'

'How? How you want me to pray for you?'

'At the altar,' he said, drawing her with him. 'Here.'

He knelt. And she, after a moment, went down beside him.

'No, not for me,' he said. 'Just pray. So I can hear you. Please.'

So she prayed, bowing her rag-wrapped head in the

hot sunlight; on the hot stone floor, before the stone altar in the open shade.

'Our Father, which are up in Heaven, hallered be Thy name. Give us today our daily bread, and give us our trespasses, as we give them to trespassers 'gainst us. Thy Kingdom come. Thy will be done. And deliver us from evil. For Thine is the kingdom, and the power, and the glory. For ever and ever. Our men.'

Then it was quite still in the church. And he whispered, at length: 'The water?'

'Dear God,' she said, 'we all poor sinners. We don't know how we going on much longer. Make it rain, dear God. You very big, dear God, and we don't look much next to you. But your world look real pretty before you take the water away, and might be you like to see it looking pretty again. I hope so, God. I only telling you because I love you. And this young fella here love you too, and he say the same. Make it rain, dear God. Bless you. Our men.'

She let her clasped hands fall to her thighs, and knelt in silence for a time. Then the diviner murmured: 'Pray for me.'

'I dunno what you want,' she said, uneasy.

'Peace,' he said. 'Just peace. Talk to him for me.' He begged her, almost.

So she prayed, uncomfortably. 'Dear God, give this young fella peace. Make him happy, God. Our men.'

Then she stood up, bowing, and moved back into the shade. But he stayed where he was, though he went on talking to her.

'There's a place for everyone,' he said. 'Isn't there? In God's kingdom.'

'Yes,' she said.

'You were told that, when you were young?'

'Yes.'

'I don't know much about it,' he confessed; still with his head bent and his back to her. 'I've found him for myself. Or he's found me.'

'You talk to him?' she asked.

'I've shouted at him,' he said, very quiet. 'What's the use? What've I done?'

He was trembling, she noticed, even in that posture.

'Did I sin before—before? Dear God, did I deserve it?'

She could not understand him. His emotions defeated her. He sounded wild, she told me, very wild. And I can imagine it. His ferocity, that had in it almost nothing of self-pity, exploded before the altar like a grenade. He had had enough, he seemed to be saying. But of what?

'I'm not—cast out,' he suddenly claimed, in a loud voice. 'If I was, I could have—I could have—ah God, what do you want me for?'

Astonishingly (I was astonished when she told me) the old woman murmured: 'One talent.'

'One talent,' he repeated, foolishly. 'One talent. Is that it?'

'Let your light shine,' she said. 'No good hiding it under a bucket. Let it shine.'

'My talent,' he said; or groaned. 'My talent.'

She would not move closer to him; but she did, with her voice, try to give comfort. 'I dunno what's wrong with you,' she said, 'but God loves you. Don't you forget it, because he don't.'

112

'What love,' he muttered. 'What love. Ah hell. My head's beating like a drum.'

He sprawled. He laid his forehead on the cool altar step, in the shade.

'You crying?' she asked him.

'No.' His answer came back muffled by the stone. 'You reckon I could?'

'Pray,' she said. 'Pray.'

'I am,' he cried. 'I have, for days, for weeks. Why am I here? Am I meant to stay? Or can I go on?' He beat on the step with his palm. 'God. God. Tell me where I stand.'

'I got to go now,' Gloria said, in a low voice.

He did not hear. She moved back to the door; seeing him, as she left, still prostrate before the altar; hearing, as she passed the empty windows, broken incoherent phrases of his pain and praying.

Byrne sang, sober and melancholy on the war memorial, a lament of his own devising.

'Tourmaline!
Red wind, red sun.
I thought I'd never come
to Tourmaline.'

So quietly his guitar grieved, as though played at the horizon. So tender, heartbreaking, his nasal tenor voice.

'In Tourmaline
the wind blows high.
The wind tears down the sky
on Tourmaline.'

113

'I wish he wouldn't sing that one,' Mary Spring said.

'Ah Tourmaline,
your walls'll fall;
doors crack, and dunes get tall
in Tourmaline.'

'Listen to the idiot,' said Kestrel.

'From Tourmaline
no news comes back;
the sand has swamped the track
to Tourmaline.'

'And yet he doesn't feel like that any more,' Tom said. 'He believes in young Michael. More than anyone.'

'Tourmaline!
Red wind, red sun.
Gone, gone—they'll never come
to Tourmaline.'

'If I say I love you,' Kestrel said, 'tonight, this minute, do I have to promise to be the same every second for the rest of my life?'

He lay in his vast brass bed. Deborah was in his arms.

'Suppose love fills your life,' he said, 'it still doesn't fill your day. There are times I forget you exist. And you do the same.'

'If that was all,' she sighed. 'Often you hate me.'

'Well, you hate me.'

'Yes, I do. When you're cross and cruel.'

'If you'd just understand that you don't own me. I'm my own property. It's good to be alone.'

'I don't think so. I don't want to be alone.'

'You're a woman,' he said—gratefully.

'Just a woman,' she said. 'There's no more to me than that.'

'It's enough for me.'

'You've got—oh, no curiosity,' she accused him. 'You don't even wonder about people. You think there's only you in the whole world.'

'It's the one thing I can be sure of.'

'And the way you treat poor Byrnie. Like an animal. And he'd die for you.'

'He's weak. Weak people've got no resistance to it.'

'Oh,' she said, wearily, 'it's a disease, is it?'

'Or a defence. Like a gecko's colour.'

She sighed for his cynicism. 'And with me, too?'

You've got to love someone. You've said so yourself, often enough.'

'And you?'

'Have we got to keep talking?'

'It's not love,' she said, 'not with you. I don't know what it is. A sort of partnership, or something. Like dancing.'

'What do you know of that's better than that?'

'I'd want to feel that—oh, that no other partner would do instead. I'd rather have the whole business go bust than have you carry it on with another woman. But you'd never feel like that.'

'Quit pretending you do.'

'I don't,' she admitted. 'I feel like a partner too. Temporary.'

'You loved me one time.'

'Oh well. "One time" isn't now.'

'So now,' he said, not quite joking, 'you love the witch-doctor.'

'I don't,' she cried, very irate. 'Why do you keep saying that?'

'I can read the signs. When we had him lying out on the road there, with his face like a horse's backside, I could see you wondering what he was going to be like. I reckon you started getting ready for him before I even opened the truck door.'

'You bastard,' said Deborah.

He laughed, like a prison gate.

'I'm not like you,' she fumed. 'Sleeping with every coloured woman in the camp—that's what you did. I'm another kind.'

'But what if you did find you loved him,' Kestrel said, suddenly very quiet and grave. 'Would you leave me?'

'I don't know,' she said. 'I s'pose I would. What would you do then?'

'I don't know either,' he said. And clasping her in his lean brown arms, he conjured her: 'Don't do it, Deb. Don't. Don't.'

I stepped out of my door to look once more at my garden. I have said before that the sky is the garden of Tourmaline.

The much-praised, the inexhaustible stars above me. Islands, ice-cold and burning. The burning ice-cold purity of God.

Love inexpressible, inexhaustible. My love for him, it, them. No matter if such love is not returned. In the

116

contemplation of stars, in the remembrance of oceans and flowers, in the voice of the lone crow and the jacaranda-blue of far ranges, I have all I need of requital.

When I think that before the world began to die I did not know this love, I can praise the manner of its dying. On the tomb of the world, ice-cold, burning, I reach out with every nerve to the ultimate purity.

Lord, fill me with your sap and make me grow.

Make me tall as karri, broad as a Moreton Bay fig. Let me shelter all Tourmaline in my shade.

Birds in the air; sheep in the far green distance.

Love, love, love; like an ache, like an emptiness. Dear God, my gold, my darling.

I could not sleep, not on such a night. So much had happened in the day to brood upon; so much had happened in the past to remember.

There was no light in Tourmaline. Pacing the road I reached the war memorial, and went beyond it to the fallen fence that marks the road's end, turning to look back. My footprints, in the moonlight, were small pits of darkness. A bottle, abandoned at the foot of the obelisk, glittered bluely. Long shadows of Tom Spring's veranda posts reached towards me. The moon was behind and to the left of the store, leaving its front, under the veranda, in deep shade; but the hotel front was lit up for two-thirds of its height, and barred diagonally with the shadows of veranda posts, each pane of the windows reflecting a moon. The iron of the roof, where the moon shone directly on it, had a curious appearance of flatness, as if the surface were no longer corrugated but a plane, striped with silver and intense black. Around all these things a faint stir of air moved, bringing a hint of freshness; but even then, even at four in the morning, one could distinguish in the cool (which is itself a scent) the smell of exhausted dust.

Mary Spring's black cat came stalking towards me, from the direction of the moon. Grotesque, the huge shadow-legs. Rubbing herself against my shins, indifferent, she accepted me without question as a feature of the night landscape.

Inside the dark houses, behind the blind windows, Tom and Mary, Kestrel and Deborah lay asleep. Moonlight would be coming in, perhaps, falling on the yellowed sheets that would be their only covering; lighting the soft curves of the women, the men's lean folded angles. I could see them, as I walked by the walls that hid them. I could feel the heat of their close houses, I could smell that bedroom smell, of shoe-leather and powder, of cloth and warm flesh, that lapped them. I believe I loved them, without wishing to interfere.

Kestrel's dog came loping to meet me, curious to know my intentions. But the cat, not to be ignored, walked back and forth in his path, brushing his face with a waving tail; so that he deserted me, after a moment, to interrogate with his nose the other animal. But from time to time, as I walked homewards, he would come bounding back, and lay his muzzle challengingly on the ground one step ahead of me.

In the iron shack behind his garden Rock would be asleep. In his tall room at the mine Jack Speed would be asleep. On the hillside, in their two stone cells, Byrne and the diviner would be asleep; stippled with moonlight, probably, from between the unmortared rocks. At the hospital, and in the house by the ruined Miner's Mess, Horse Carson and others would be sleeping; and outside their humpies, dogs by their sides, the natives. And ten miles away, by their stock route well, Dave Speed and Jimmy Bogada lay, presumably, under the stars.

Remembering the natives' stories (unsubstantiated) of lone men savaged by dingoes, and their use of protective campfires, it occurred to me that now, in this country, in this drought, there is nothing whatsoever to fear.

Church and bell tower on their small hill stood out black against the luminous horizon. Police station and gaol glimmered, very pale, in the moonlight. Behind me, in the Springs' yard, the rooster flapped and crowed; and Kestrel's dog, leaping about, forequarters low to the ground, gave for my benefit a yap of mock alarm.

It came to me suddenly that man is a disease of God; and that God must surely die.

There is a book I remember, from the days of my schooling; a child's book, a school book, from which I began (I didn't succeed) to learn French. And it had a picture that haunts me still. I knew that picture long before I could read, for the book had been my mother's, and I was struck, as illiterate children are, by the strange image. So for years I returned and returned to it.

There was a well beneath a great tree. And in the tree was a princess, in hiding. And by the well, a hideous, pathetic, ludicrous negress, with a pitcher on her shoulder.

The negress was gazing into the well; which reflected not her, but the face of the princess among the leaves. The black woman's vast teeth showed in delight.

'*Ah, comme je suis belle!' s'écria la négresse.*

A joke, then—was it?

Oh you in the branches.

I don't find that funny.

EIGHT

Byrne pushed the swinging door and went into the bar. No one was there. The door was cutting the sunlight into strips and dropping them on the floor. Imprisoned flies were crying.

He went on, through the stark dining room, to the kitchen where Deborah was drying dishes.

'Where's Kes?' he asked her.

'Sleeping,' she said, turning her head, a willow-pattern plate in one hand, the same blue as her dress, and a tea-towel made of Kestrel's shirt in the other.

'Lazy sod.'

'He and Tom are the only ones who work in this town,' she said. 'Why shouldn't he sometimes?'

'I want a drink.'

'I thought you'd stopped it.'

'I feel good,' he said. 'It's when I feel good I mostly need it. I feel so good I'll bust if I don't calm down.'

'You can't wake him up. And he'll clobber you if you take it.'

'I can't help that.'

'Well, you can't say I gave it to you, anyway.'

He leaned in the doorway, watching her. Beyond her, through the high sash window, lay the courtyard of the hotel, a veranda on three sides, the fourth wall made up of an iron shed. Warped crates and crumbling cartons were piled on the slate paving of the yard, and dust-coated bottles of extraordinary antiquity. The shed was actually a garage, a museum for a dead utility.

'It looks as if no one lives here,' he said. The dusty windows were stone blind.

'It feels like it too,' she said, opening a cupboard and putting the plates away. Then she combed her hair in front of a greenish mirror, and turned back to pick up a bulging flourbag from the table.

'What's that?' he idly asked.

'Bread,' she said.

'Going visiting?'

'He won't ask for anything. You have to offer it to him. Is he up there, in the hut?'

'I think he is. He's not too keen on visitors, but.'

'I can't help that,' she said, echoing him. 'I bet you're there half the time.'

The light from the doorway lit one side of his poor cratered face. 'You reckon I'm a nuisance?' he asked, anxiously.

'No,' she said, 'no. You're too touchy. If he doesn't want to see you he doesn't want to see anyone.'

That made him happier, and he grinned at her, hollow-cheeked.

'I'll come with you,' he offered.

'Oh, why?' she said. 'He won't talk unless there's no one else there and he has to. Let me go by myself. All right?'

He gave in. 'All right.' But he looked dispirited as he trailed after her, through the bare-floored empty dining room and into the droning bar.

'I warn you,' she said, as he went behind the bar-counter.

'Okay,' he said, 'you warned me,' watching her through the doors. Then he reached for a bottle and poured himself a drink.

The flies in the traps irrepressibly sizzled on. The clock, with a view of Windsor Castle on the glass over the pendulum, announced the seconds from a distance of twenty minutes. He leaned on the bar, his forehead on his hand, black-nailed fingers in his stiff black hair.

In time he roused himself, tossing off the contents of the glass; and taking bottle and glass with him he went out, through the bread-smelling kitchen, across the derelict yard, to his monastic room with its sagging iron bed.

Looking out of my window I saw her coming, little puffs of dust rising from her bare feet. So I came out of my house and waited for her at my gate. Oh Lord, I am like a spider nowadays; like a spider that lives on news.

'Where are you bound?' I asked her, as she came up. I thought she might be coming to see me; but why should she?

123

'To Michael's place,' she said. 'He doesn't come down, so he never gets any bread.'

'It's hot,' I said.

'It's the same every day,' she replied.

'Sad to be old in this country; not even the weather to talk about.'

She said, indifferently: 'I can't imagine anything else.'

'I wonder what you'll talk about when you're my age. Before, even when nothing happened, there was always the weather—changing—reminding you of the universe. You won't have that.'

'I'll talk about my grandchildren,' she said.

'Ah, you'll have grandchildren?'

'Why not?' she asked, with her eyes suddenly wide and questioning. 'Why shouldn't I? I must.'

'Are there any children in Tourmaline?'

'Yes,' she said; or hotly affirmed. 'In the camp. There must be. One or two.'

'I suppose there must be. I never go there.'

'You should.' She sounded annoyed with me. 'They're people too.'

'I get tired. It's a long walk.'

She stood with the bag dangling in her hand, red dust on her ankles, frowning, thinking. She was looking at my gaol but not seeing it. At last she said: 'It *is* hot,' as if to please me.

'Shall I come with you?'

'Everyone wants to come with me,' she said.

'Ah well, I won't, then.'

'You're not hurt, are you? Only, he won't talk if you come.'

124

'I don't mind,' I said; adding: 'He's an interesting boy.'

'He's not a boy,' she objected. 'He's been somewhere.'

'So he has. But where?'

'He might tell me, if I'm clever.'

'You'll find it hard.'

'Well,' she murmured, with a shrug. And she looked away, over my gaol, to the hillside where his hut squatted, indistinguishable among the rocks.

'Will you come in,' I said, 'and have some tea or something?' But she politely refused, swinging the bag in her hand.

So we took leave of one another. And I went back to my kitchen, where the kettle boiled on the rusty stove, and a solitary fly on the window crossed and recrossed her distant figure climbing the hillside.

He was asleep when she got there; sprawled asleep on the iron bed with the grey broad-striped blanket, hiding his eyes in the crook of one arm. She put her flourbag down on the packing case and studied him. In the red light of the hut his skin was like copper. His feet were bare. He showed no sign of waking.

She stood over him, smiling her rather secret smile. Then she reached out and began to tickle the soles of his feet.

He sighed in his sleep. Suddenly there was a halt in his breathing, and he was awake, sitting up in alarm, his strangely coloured eyes staring.

'Hell, you scared me,' he said at length, lying back again and breathing out heavily through his nostrils. 'Excuse me a minute. My heart hasn't found its way home yet.'

'You *are* a nervous man,' said Deborah.

'Must have been dreaming. Can't remember.'

She sat down on the foot of the bed, looking up his body to his red-ochre face. And he, with his hands behind his head, watched her, guardedly.

'Is your town as lazy as Tourmaline?' she asked him. 'Everybody's asleep this afternoon.'

'What else is there to do?'

'Well, there's your gold.'

'It can wait.'

'And the water.'

'I'm not ready,' he said, with his sudden rather aggressive curtness.

'Are you all right now?'

'All right?'

'Your head, and so on. D'you still get those headaches?'

'Now and again,' he said. 'I'll survive.'

'I think you've got one now. Why are you frowning?'

'It's nothing. Forget it.'

'Let me rub your forehead,' she said, moving to rise. 'That helps. I do that for Mary.'

But he alerted himself instantly, and sat for a moment on the edge of the bed with his face in his hands, before looking up again with a rather petulant half-laugh and a shake of the head. 'Are all women like this?' he wondered. 'Look, I'm a big boy. Don't mother me.'

She scrutinized him; intrigued, but still ironical. 'You are—you're extraordinary,' she said at last. 'I don't know any people like you.'

He grinned. 'As you say. But you don't know many people, do you?'

126

'You're as cold as a fish.'

'Ah well,' he said, with his hands on his blue thighs, unfolding himself, and standing, and wandering to the packing case, 'how many fish have you seen, anyway?'

'None,' she admitted. 'So what? Why do you hate people to touch you?'

'You're raving,' he said; but without any particular discourtesy, or even interest. 'And if you weren't it wouldn't be your business. What's this?'

'It's bread. That I made for you. But if you want to be independent you can always chuck it down the nearest shaft.'

'There's no denying it,' he said (with a certain embarrassment), 'you're a kind-hearted girl. And I wish you'd stop doing me favours.'

'Why?'

'Because I can't do any for you.'

'That's not the reason.'

'Now look,' he said, 'how well do you think you know me?'

'You don't want people to do you favours because you don't want them near enough to know you. But you can't get away with it. There's hardly one person in Tourmaline that hasn't done something for you.'

He looked at her in astonishment, and remarked, after thinking about it: 'That's a cold sort of mind you've got. Like a fish.'

'We're a pair of fish, then.'

'Stranded in Tourmaline. A miracle.'

'I love you,' she said. With great pain.

127

Then he was frozen—staring. But not quite frozen. Because he began to tremble.

'I want to sleep with you,' she said.

He was frozen.

At last he brought himself to move, thrusting his shaking hands deep into his trouser-pockets, and retreated (trying to make a casual movement of it, but a retreat it was) to the further wall. He propped himself there, looking down. He would not look at her, although she never ceased to watch him, with her eyes bright and sombre, humble and defiant, all at the same time. When at last he would speak she saw that his lips were trembling, in a very strange way, like the lips of a cat that is stalking an insect, and his voice was deadened as if his vocal chords had been seized up with ice. 'What are you?' he demanded, frozen and trembling. 'A harlot?'

As it happened that was a word she knew. And she cried to him: 'No, no, I'm not. I'm honest. I love you.' She was humble and defiant, brilliant and sombre.

'Ah,' he said, 'you're like an animal, you hot bitch. Go home to your husband.'

'He's not my husband.'

'Of course he is, in the sight of God.'

'What do you know about the sight of God?'

'More than you think, maybe.'

She tossed her head, a wild meaningless gesture. She was trying not to cry, perhaps. 'I can't love him. He won't let me. You know him, you can believe that, can't you?'

'So you thought you'd come to me?'

She said, quite simply: 'I want to have your baby.'

He sounded sick, with rage or disgust. 'What makes you think you can talk this—filth to me? Did you think I was the sort of man who'd listen to it?'

'I can't understand you,' she burst out. 'I'm honest, that's all. And why are you frightened?'

'Frightened?' he said. 'Me?'

'You're shaking.'

'I'm cold. That's all.'

'But it's hot, it's roasting. This hut's like an oven.'

'After hell, anywhere's cold,' he said. 'And black.'

'Always hell, hell, hell. Where is it? Is there such a thing?'

'Under your feet,' he said, with cold conviction. 'And you'll burn. All Tourmaline.'

'What have we done?' she protested. 'Tom and Mary burn? I don't believe it.'

'Forgotten God's law,' he said; remote, pontifical. 'For the sake of some law of their own. And others'll burn for the sins of the flesh, or for blasphemy, or just for not listening. Or at least, they would have done——'

'But *you* came?'

He repeated it, in a dead voice. 'But I came.'

Slowly she rose from the bed, smoothing her skirt, hoping, perhaps, by her movement to bring him to acknowledge her physical presence and forgive her. But still he would not look at her.

'What'll I do?' she asked, in despair.

'Take your bread. I don't want it.'

'I don't mean that. I mean, about hell, about sin. How do I know what to believe. Tom says one thing, you say another thing. Kes says: 'Bull' to both of you. Maybe nobody's right.'

'Yes, somebody is,' he said. 'I am.'

She gave a little fretful laugh, reaching for the bag with the bread in. 'How do you know?'

And at last he looked up. 'Because God's spoken to me,' he told her, with eyes like blue glass.

She came home again; hurt, broken. No one was in the bar. The flies were disturbed, and cried, when she tossed her bag of bread on the bar-counter.

Kestrel heard her footstep, and called out from the bedroom. So she went, stiff and slow, to where he was, lying naked and sweating on the vast bed, his hands behind his head, staring at the flaking ceiling in a kind of trance.

The room was curtained and shadowy. Her tawny skin, his olive skin, glimmered in the dim light. He smelled of clean sweat.

'Where've you been?' he asked, turning his head on the pillow.

'Nowhere.'

'There's a lot of nowhere round Tourmaline.'

'You know where I've been,' she said.

'I don't know why, yet.'

'To take him some bread.'

'Uh-huh,' he said. 'And how was he?'

'He was asleep. Like every other useless bastard in this bloody town.'

'Hey, hey. Mary never taught you those words.'

'Oh, leave me alone.'

130

'Come here,' he said, 'Little Red Riding Hood. The wolf's got something for you.'

'You make me sick,' she burst out, half-weeping; and ran away from him out to the kitchen, where she sat down at the table and hid her face in her arms.

In his own good time he came after her, shirtless, and stood behind her chair. Her neck was cool and smooth as chalcedony, and little hairs that had escaped from her pony tail were straggling on it. He put his lips against her neck, and would have kissed her; but she made an impatient movement, so he blew a raspberry instead.

Then she did weep, in real rage.

'What's up?' he asked. 'What did you bring the bread back for?'

'Go away,' she said.

'Did he make a pass at you?'

'No! Go away!'

'Did you make a pass at him?'

'You make me sick,' she cried again.

'Don't get off your bike,' he said. 'I've just got a thirst for knowledge, that's all.'

'He doesn't eat bread. It's against his religion.'

He couldn't help himself then. He roared with laughter.

'Because the wheat's sick,' she went on, wildly. 'Like everything out there. You know what the Law says. D'you think that's funny? You're mad.'

'Is that the only thing that's against his religion?'

'For God's sake,' she pleaded, lifting her head, and scowling and weeping at him both together. 'Do you have to keep cackling like an old chook right in my ear?'

'Ah, she's a funny girl,' he said; 'she's a humorist.' He put his hand on her shoulder, affectionately.

And she got up, knocking over the chair, and escaped from him into the yard, running through the dusty bottles.

He strolled after her. She could not go far.

'Oh look,' she called, half-laughing, in a shaky way. 'He's asleep too. What a dead town. With his damn boots on the quilt. I'll murder him.'

It was Byrne she meant. The door of his little room was open, but nothing could be seen of him, only the soles of his boots against the iron bed-foot; which was painted white, but flaking, holding pockets of red dust in its bald patches.

'Let him sleep,' Kestrel said. 'Who wants him?'

'I do,' she said. 'I don't want to talk to you. Byrnie!'

'You stupid bitch,' he said, with affection. 'What's got into you? All right, if you want him.' And he stooped to pick up a small stone from the yard, and tossed it through the door to lob on Byrne's stomach.

The boots didn't move.

'I didn't mean chuck boondies at him,' Deborah objected. 'Why do you have to treat him like that?'

'He didn't even feel it,' Kestrel said. Then the dark suspicion came down on him, wiping the grin from his curling mouth. 'Is he pissed?'

'How'd I know?' she demanded. But she hesitated.

'By Jesus, if he's been helping himself you won't murder him, I will.'

'Leave him alone—please, Kes. Or wait till he's sober.'

'Why should I?' He had grown darker, and his grey eyes paler, uncanny. He started to come towards Byrne's door.

But she was ahead of him, shaking Byrne, calling: 'Wake up, Byrnie,' while Byrne groaned and stirred. 'Kes is after you. Wake up.'

The black eyes dragged open, under the devilish eyebrows, in the dark spoiled face. He was dazed. He was more than that, he was drunk as a skunk. 'What? What?' he was saying, with a rum bottle beside him, under his armpit, and the stinking liquor soaking his shirt and the quilt beneath. 'What's Kes want?'

'Your blood,' Kestrel said, quietly, studying him from the doorway. 'Ah Christ, wouldn't he make you puke? My cousin. You're a credit to your upbringing, boy.'

'Get out, Byrnie,' Deborah was whispering. 'Quick.'

He dragged himself to his feet, and stood with his head hanging and his eyes closed, swaying a little. Then: 'No good,' he said. 'I've had it.' He sat down on the edge of the bed.

'So you helped yourself again,' Kestrel said, in his stillest and smallest voice.

'Couldn't wake you, Kes.'

'That was a kind thought.'

'Didn't want to be a nuisance. Nuisance to too many people.'

'Come out here,' Kestrel said.

'Don't you,' Deborah said. 'You stay here.'

'You shut up,' Kestrel said to her. 'Come here, laddie.'

'I won't let you go, Byrnie,' Deborah said, grabbing him by the belt.

'Got to go,' Byrne said, breaking away from her and shambling to the door, from which Kestrel had retreated to

133

wait for him in the yard. 'What d'you want, Kes?' he was asking, coming to him, and swaying slightly when he stood.

Then Kestrel hit him across the cheekbone with the back of his hand. And as Byrne simply stood there, shaking his head, he hit him again on the other cheek.

'Hit him back, Byrnie,' Deborah cried from the door. 'Why do you let him do it? Hit him.'

''S all right, Deb,' Byrne said. ''S all right. I was asking for it. I deserved it.'

At that point Kestrel gave him a straight right to the head, and he went down, gushing blood from the nostrils.

'You dingo,' Deborah said to Kestrel, with extraordinary contempt and conviction. 'He's drunk.'

'Well, now,' said Kestrel.

And Byrne, on the slate paving of the yard, kept muttering: ''S all right, Deb, 's all right.'

'Have you done enough now?' Deborah enquired. 'Why don't you go and do something interesting, like pulling the legs off flies?'

And Kestrel, all the time, was standing over Byrne, with those pale eyes of his, and thin bent lips like the seagulls in a child's drawing.

'Get up,' he said.

''S over now, Kes,' Byrne said. 'Want to sleep now.'

'Get up.'

'Can't, Kes.'

So Kestrel knelt beside him, grabbing him by the shirt collar, and talking very quietly. 'I've had enough,' he said. 'It makes me feel pretty proud, seeing you like this—what do *you* think?' And his soft anger was terrible, because of the hysteria underneath it. 'Some day I won't know when to stop. I'll kill you, that's for sure.'

'Sorry, Kes, sorry,' Byrne was muttering.

'Why do you keep tempting me? Ah, you shit!'

'Sorry, Kes.'

'Why don't you die? Why don't you just die? What good are you to anyone? Why don't you just drop dead?'

'Oh, stop it,' Deborah called out, weeping again, with pity and indignation. 'What good are you, or anyone? Leave him alone, Kes. You'll make him kill himself.'

'Why don't you die,' Kestrel said, almost pleading, in a tone like incantation. 'You stink already. Go on, Billy boy, die for us.'

'I hope God will strike you dead,' said Deborah, sincerely.

'You stink,' Kestrel said again; and stood up.

'Poor Byrnie,' Deborah wept. 'I wish you'd get up and kill him.'

But Byrne could only lie there, on his side, with his blood on the paving and his poor abject eyes bemused, wondering what had happened. ''S all right,' he kept saying. 'I was asking for it. I might hit him if I wasn't, but I was asking for it.'

'*You* hit me?' Kestrel said, laughing. And he suddenly kicked Byrne, in the belt buckle or thereabouts, and went away, rather fast.

Byrne, clutching his stomach, coughing and groaning, got to his feet somehow, and staggered across to a veranda post, where he supported himself. He began to vomit.

And Deborah came towards him, weeping her generous tears.

'Don't,' he managed to gasp out. 'Don't come near me. I stink. I've spewed all down my strides.'

'What does that matter?' she said, holding his thin shoulders till his breath came back.

'Ah hell,' he said at last. 'I shouldn't have done it.'

'Byrnie, Byrnie,' she said, half-laughing, half-crying, 'you're a saint, and a bloody fool.'

'I know I'm a fool,' he said.

'You could buy all the grog in his bar. You're rich, Byrnie.'

'How?'

'From the gold. From Michael's reef.'

'Forgot that,' he said, without elation.

'*He* didn't forget. He knew damn well all the time.'

'Mistake,' Byrne said.

'No, it wasn't.'

'He'll get over it. I'll go home for a while.'

They stood among the crates, the bottles, the blind eyes of the dusty windows.

'Don't go up there,' she said. 'You're too drunk anyway. Go to Tom and Mary.'

'Not like this. What'd Mary think of me?'

'They'd rather see you like that than never see you again.'

He turned round, wiping his mouth, and looked at her, hopeful. 'You reckon?'

'Your friends'd do a lot for you. And you've got plenty.'

'All right,' he said, 'I'll go there, for tonight. Ah, but,' he said, shaking his head and grimacing in disgust, 'God, I'm a dirty bastard. A dirty bastard.'

'Go to Tom,' she said after him, as he crossed the yard. 'Go straight there.'

And he muttered 'Okay', disappearing through the little alley between the hotel and the tin garage.

When he had gone the valiant girl, with the blood of her mother's mothers working (no doubt) at pretty high pressure in her veins, stooped to pick up a bottle. It was a very old bottle, one of those green ones with a deep concave base, and it was furry with ancient dust.

She grasped the neck in her right hand, and went into the kitchen, where Kestrel was sitting at the table. He did not look round.

'Is he all right?' he asked, with a faint suggestion of remorse.

'He's all right,' she said. And as she spoke the bottle descended. She was surprised that it didn't break.

He went over like a shot emu.

After pausing to make sure he wasn't dead, she went into the bedroom and collected up her clothes. Then she crossed the road, appearing beside Byrne at the store counter.

'Well, well, well,' said Tom, all luminous. 'Clothes too, this time?'

'I'm here forever,' she said. 'Poor Pa.'

NINE

I suppose that this day (a day of extraordinary activity for Deborah) might have ended tragically. But as it happened Kestrel was able to pick himself up before very long, and stagger off to his bed and lay himself out there, with a groan and a curse or two, to recover. And presently Bill the Dill and Pete Macaroni, coming in search of a drink, thought to look for him in the bedroom, and so became the first to hear the news of his misfortune.

It was a shock to Bill. 'She never crowned you?' he said, marvelling. 'Bloody hell.'

But Pete thought it was funny.

'You can laugh,' said Kestrel, with his eyes closed, scowling.

'Wait till I tell Horse,' Pete said. 'He'll split himself.'

'Why would she do that?' Bill wanted to know. 'Was you belting her or something?'

'I never laid a flicking finger on her. She came up behind and dropped me with a bottle.'

'They get like that,' said Pete, who was married to Darleen Bogada. 'It's in the blood.'

'I'd like to see Shirl try it on,' said Bill; meaning Shirley Yandana, his wife.

'Give me a woman with spirit,' said Kestrel; still in some pain.

'You try Darleen's sister next time,' Bill advised. 'She took a chunk out of Charlie's ear once.'

'Ah, nick off,' said Kestrel. 'I'm a married man. Where is she?'

'Deb?'

'Is she in the bar?'

'No, no one there.'

'Hell,' said Kestrel, putting his hands to his painful eyes, 'she's gone to Mary.'

'I'll go and get her,' Pete offered.

'She wouldn't come. Tomorrow, maybe.'

'Well, what are you going to do about your head?'

'Sleep it off,' Kestrel said. 'Pub's shut. Sorry.'

There was a sound of voices in the bar, and tramping feet advancing. Presently Horse Carson and Dicko appeared.

'Go home,' Kestrel groaned. 'I'm wounded.'

'Deb laid him out with a bottle,' Bill explained, sympathetically.

'Shouldn't have done that,' Horse said. 'Wasting the stuff.'

'It was empty,' said Kestrel.

They stood by the bedside, the four of them, grinning and commiserating.

'Has she gone for good, Kes?' Dicko asked.

'God,' he said, 'I hope not. No, she wouldn't do that.'

'All the same,' said Pete, 'looks like she ain't too pleased with you.'

'I'll bring her over,' Horse said. 'Saw her going into the store half an hour back.'

'Better wear your tin hat,' said Dicko.

'Bloody vultures,' Kestrel said. 'You'd be laughing if you got hit, I'll bet.'

'D'you want me to go over there?'

'You can try,' Kestrel said, with no great hope. So Horse went away, with a great smirk on his face, like a dry creekbed in the desert.

When he appeared at the back door of the store Mary and Deborah were together in the kitchen. Mary was ironing, using a rusty flat-iron of Tom's mother's. Its mate was heating on the stove. Deborah was sitting on a kitchen chair, silent, restored to her habitual stillness, and rather knocked over, perhaps, by the draining heat of the room. She looked up at Horse without any expression, but she knew why he had come.

'You made a mess of Kes,' he said.

'He asked for it.'

'You might have killed him.'

Her fathomless eyes agreed. 'Might have.'

'Might have what?' Mary asked, putting down the iron on a metal plate.

'Killed him,' said Deborah. 'I hit him.'

'With a bottle,' said Horse. 'And laid him out.'

Mary looked at Deborah as if they'd not been introduced. Then: 'I'm surprised at you,' she said, gravely.

'He was hitting Byrnie,' Deborah said, 'and then he kicked him. I might have kicked *him* after that, but he wasn't awake to appreciate it.'

And Mary stood marvelling, with her soft greying hair escaping from the loose bun and trailing on her damp forehead.

Horse said to Deborah: 'Will you come and look after him?'

'No,' she said; quietly, but with complete finality.

'Really,' Mary said, 'I think you ought to. You can't knock people down with bottles and just leave them there.'

'He can stay there and the ants can eat him alive,' said Deborah, 'for all I care.'

'Fair go,' said Horse, a bit shocked.

'I used to hate him sometimes,' she said, 'but now he just makes me sick. Tell him that.'

'You mean,' said Horse, 'you're not going back?'

'Not ever. If he hasn't guessed that yet, I must have really done something to his head.'

Mary's plump and bare forearms were behind her, untying apron strings. 'You're not to be vindictive,' she said. 'I wouldn't have thought it was in you.'

'Do you *want* me to go back, then?'

'You know I don't. But still——'

'Don't cry for him. He's not a man. He's partly a baby, and the rest of him's a wild animal.'

'But we'll have to do something about him.'

'That's what I say,' said Horse.

'What can we do?' Deborah asked. 'Give Horse a few pills for his headache and let's forget about him.'

'If you won't go,' said Mary, 'I'll have to.'

'Oh dear,' said Deborah, wryly smiling. 'He'll love that.'

'You don't leave me much choice,' said Mary, taking off her apron and hanging it behind the door. She opened a cupboard which was, among other things, her medicine closet, and looked to see what there was to offer. Not much, apparently, beyond a few aspirin that the diviner had left her.

'Well, Horse,' she said, pocketing these, 'lead on. Will you finish the ironing, Deborah?'

'All right.'

'And get tea for Tom and Byrnie if I'm not back?'

'Byrnie won't wake up for hours.'

'Then you'd better wake him. He probably hasn't eaten all day.'

'I wish I could feel kind to everybody,' said Deborah, in a low voice.

'Well, I suppose Kes has been pretty nasty.'

'He's a snake,' said Deborah. 'I don't know why someone like Horse doesn't jump on him.'

'I got nothing against him,' Horse said. 'Leave me out of this.'

'Oh sure,' she said, bitterly, 'you get your grog from him. What can anyone do?' And she got up, brooding, and put the cooling iron back on the stove.

'Be good,' said Mary. And she went away, following Horse across the road, while the tall and savage girl reached for her apron.

Dicko had gone by the time Mary arrived, but there was a sort of picnic going on in the bedroom, with Bill

142

stretched out on the bed beside Kestrel and Pete sprawled across the foot of it, glasses in their hands, talking in a cheery manner to the invalid; who lay glooming with closed eyes, unresponsive. They were a bit taken aback to see Mary; especially Kestrel.

'How do you feel?' she asked, coming round to his side of the bed.

'I feel bloody,' he said. 'Where did that girl learn to belt her husband?'

She put her hand on his dark brow.

'Look,' he said, 'I haven't got a temperature, I can tell you before you start. I've just got a dirty great emu egg on the back of my skull.'

'Don't be impatient,' said Mary.

'Where is the bitch?'

'She's not coming back to you,' Mary said. 'And if you use that language to me, I'll slap you. I'm old enough to be your mother.'

'The skies are falling,' he groaned. 'You let one woman hit you and they all start. She doesn't mean it.'

'She certainly does.'

'You'd be sure to say that.'

'I think she's dinkum,' Horse said. 'If she isn't, she's giving a bloody good imitation of a dame that hates your guts.'

'I can't think of a woman,' said Mary, offhand, 'who doesn't. What can I do for you?'

'You can't do anything.'

'Will I make you a cup of tea?'

'That would be lovely,' said Kestrel, crushingly.

'I don't know why I came,' Mary said.

'Why don't you shut up, Kes,' Horse suggested, 'and give your head a rest. And Mary's.'

'Why don't you go home?'

Mary said: 'Now, that is an idea. Pete, Bill, get off his bed and make tracks.'

'Bossiest woman in Tourmaline,' Bill complained. But he did get up, lazy and tousled, and lounged in the doorway emptying his glass. People tended to be obedient when Mary took charge.

Pete, for the sake of his self-esteem as man and husband, made an effort at passive resistance; but Horse, with his passion for throwing people about, seized the opportunity and hauled him off by one leg. So Kestrel was left in sole possession of the huge bed, and lay there in gloomy state, his eyes closed and screwed up with pain and his shirtless torso heaving. 'Why doesn't everyone go?' he asked. 'I'm not sick, I'm just ropeable. Stay away from me.'

'We'll have a nice cup of tea,' Mary said, to irritate him, 'just the two of us. Go on, you men, shoo.' And she drove them before her, like sheep, until she had seen the bar door swing after them and knew that the business of spreading the news through Tourmaline was under way. Then she went back to the bedroom.

Under the flaking ceiling, like a map of Mars, Kestrel lay staring. The big dim room was bare, had a camped-in look. He still kept his boots on. With the steely quality of his fine dark face and bent mouth went a certain forlornness.

'I don't need anything, Mary,' he said, as she came back.

'You need to eat and drink,' she supposed, 'like anyone else.'

'Hurts me to accept a favour.'

'Don't think I'm not enjoying my Christian revenge.'

He grinned, turning his head on the pillow, towards plump Mary with her brown ironical eyes. 'Well, I could call you my mother-in-law, sort of. One of the family.'

'Not any more,' she said. 'I'm sorry, Kes. For you, that is.'

'She's set on not coming back?'

'You couldn't drag her.'

'She'll go to the witch-doctor,' he said; not with resentment or as an accusation, but almost idly, as if recalling dull history.

'To——? Oh, to Michael. No. Why on earth do you say that?'

'You'll see,' he said.

She felt some pity for him. And she said sitting on the edge of the bed: 'Kes, I've never been your enemy. I've been fond of you sometimes. You were a likely boy, in lots of ways.'

'I haven't changed. What you don't like in me now was there then.'

'I know it was. And I didn't exactly admire you, even in those days. I'll tell you why, if you like.'

'I know myself,' he said. 'Better than you can.'

'You're greedy,' she said. 'And selfish. And cruel. You're cold, and you use people—as far as anyone can in Tourmaline.'

'You'll have me falling in love with myself,' he said.

'Do you have to be like that?'

'I do,' he said, not very happily. And he went on, with astonishing candour: 'I might be the sanest bloke in Tourmaline, I wouldn't be surprised, but I have my days of wanting to run amok. I can't breathe here. I want to bash the walls down and get some air. What the hell is there for a man like me to do? Is this all the life there is? I just can't face another thirty-five years of suffocating. I can tell you now, even Deb was a kind of suffocating to me. She wanted to put a fence round me. Some days I just about couldn't stand it; but hell, if you're going to suffocate you might as well do it in good company. Does any of that make sense?'

'No,' she said.

'It didn't to Deb, either. But that's the story of my life.'

He was covering his eyes with the back of his hand; an irritable, but also a childlike gesture.

'That tea,' Mary said, rising. 'And those aspirin for your head. I shouldn't have started you talking.'

'Should be honoured. Not an easy thing to do.'

'And some food. I'll get to work.'

'So I'll be alone tonight,' he said. 'Like old times.'

'Will you be all right?'

'Don't be silly—what do you think?'

'Byrnie could come, probably. He should be in a fit state by now.'

'He'll be lucky,' Kestrel said. 'But send him, anyway. I want to see him.'

' "Send him",' she mimicked. 'You think he's your dog.'

'I reckon he's happy to be like that,' Kestrel said. And he lay glooming, brooding, with his eyes turned to the maps of undiscovered planets that covered the ceiling, and the quick thoughts moving under the mask; a disturbance.

And Byrne did come, later; not by any means in a healthy condition, or quite sober, but well-disposed, as always. There was a lamp beside the bed, throwing light upwards at him and making great mountains and pits of the topography of his face. His black eyes shone from circles of darkness. He was both sympathetic and placating, ready to shoulder all responsibility for Kestrel's mishap. If Deborah had been there, she would have been irritated beyond bearing.

Kestrel looked at him expressionlessly, or almost. But Byrne, who was sensitive to such things and had a good deal of experience, could see that he was being regarded as a mean sort of object whose existence was somehow regrettable; and what could one expect the poor fool to do but apologize?

So he said: 'I'm sorry about that, Kes.'

'Ah, drop it,' said Kestrel.

And Byrne stood humbly waiting, over the lamp.

After a time: 'Have you seen her?' Kestrel asked.

'Yair, we've been talking.'

'And she won't come back?'

'I don't know. Give her a while and she might.'

'You really think that?'

'Don't think there's much chance. But I can't make her out, and that's a fact. She could do anything.'

'You're not wrong,' Kestrel said. 'Well, sit down, for Christ's sake, you're making me tired.'

So Byrne sat himself on the edge of the bed; light

filling the craters and hollows of his face, making him look harmless again.

'I treated you rough,' Kestrel brought himself to admit.

'Forget it,' Byrne said.

'I've got a temper. You know that.'

'Sure, I know it. Better than anyone else does, I'd say.'

Kestrel made no answer to that. And he lay for some minutes in silence, not looking at Byrne but staring at the ceiling, while the room filled with peculiar tensions. Although his mask was blank, something was boiling in him. He tried to control it, closing his eyes.

But Byrne, sitting there, miserably, studying his own hands resting on his thighs, knew about it. And he said, without looking up: 'Why do you hate me, Kes? What did I do, and when did I do it?'

'I don't know,' Kestrel said.

Byrne gave a broken laugh. 'What you mean is, I'm the sort of bloke people just naturally can't stick. There doesn't have to be any other reason. Is that it?'

He turned his head to look at the face on the pillow. He was resigned. Abject is the word that cannot be avoided when speaking of poor Byrnie.

And Kestrel, shifting his shoulders impatiently, burst out: 'Why've you got to be so flicking humble?'

'Sorry.'

'Christ, there you go again.'

'It's a nervous habit,' Byrne said.

'Can't you fight me back, sometimes?'

'Too late to start now.'

'Listen,' Kestrel said, urgently. 'Listen. I can't help

148

myself. If you go crawling around me, I can't help it, I've got to kick you. And listen, I'm getting scared. I'm dangerous. Someday I'm going to do you an injury. You'd better stay away. I warn you.'

He was breathing hard. And Byrne's face was turned away, watching his hands, his mouth stretched tight by some emotion or other.

'Are you listening to me?'

'Yair,' said Byrne.

'You got nothing to say?'

'I want to die,' Byrne said, with a laugh that came like blood from a wound. His eyes were blind.

'Keep away from me,' Kestrel said.

'If you say so.'

'It isn't my fault. I didn't make myself.'

'You made me,' Byrne said, softly.

But Kestrel had no reply for that. So he lay there, Byrne sat there, in separate silences, and the lamp burned on, and in the dimness the great bulks of wardrobes and dressing-table and chest-of-drawers against the walls stubbornly endured. There are these moments, when the duration of objects appears positive, when it comes to seem an act of indomitable will.

At last Kestrel asked: 'Where is she?'

'In the store,' Byrne said.

'I mean, where's she sleeping?'

'In that back room, where Mike was.'

'I'll go and talk to her. It might be the last time.'

'You ought to lie down, with that head.'

'I'm all right,' Kestrel said. 'You go home and sleep that liquor off.'

And the lamp burned on; the furniture endured.

'Well, so long,' said Byrne, in a trance; and got up and went out, through the lightless bar.

The window of Deborah's room was open, and the moon shone through it, making black valleys and snow-capped ranges of the white coverlet under which she lay; striping the white-washed corrugated iron of the walls, glittering in the cracked glaze of the rose-adorned basin and ewer. The old curtains hung still. Then Kestrel, putting one leg over the sill, disturbed them.

She was awake, and sat up. Her face, in the moonlight, was quite serene.

'Go home,' she said.

He hissed at her. 'Keep quiet, girl.'

'I don't care who hears,' she said; but she did keep her voice down, and in fact didn't speak at all while he was making his way across the room and sitting himself down on the bed. The moon shone all the while in her deep eyes. Two moons. He looked at them, glowing there in her calm face.

'They've been coming one after another,' he said, 'and telling me you've gone for good.'

She said nothing.

'What do you say?'

'It's true,' she said, indifferently.

'You don't like me now?'

'I never did like you,' she said. 'I loved you for a while, but that was different.'

'If you'd tell me what way you want me to be, I might manage it. I could change, maybe.'

She sighed, to show her patience. 'It's just *you* I don't like. You're so—*mean*.'

'What way? Because I hit Byrnie?'

'Oh, what's the good of talking?' she protested. 'Yes, it's that, partly. But mostly not anything you do. Just that you don't do anything.'

'I get it,' he said. 'I should go divining.'

'Or something. Anything.'

'Well, I might,' he said, darkly watching her.

'It won't make any difference to me. I know you now.'

That made him angry. 'You,' he said, 'know me. Don't kid yourself.'

And she laughed, without a sound, showing her white teeth to the moon.

'Listen,' he said, reaching out and holding her by the shoulders. 'Listen,' he said; and then would not go on, but bent his black head and hid his face against her neck.

She said, without moving: 'Go home.'

'I love you,' he said, into her skin. 'Love you, Deb, love you.'

She pushed him away with a sudden thrust, and got out of the bed, and stood for a moment in the middle of the floor, in the flooding moonlight, as if she were thinking. She was naked, all gleam and shadow, rusty steel and impenetrable darkness, cool as quartz.

'What are you trying to do to me?' he whispered, half-sprawled on the bed.

'Nothing,' she said, reaching behind the door for a dressing-gown, of yellowish colour, which she put on. 'I can't sleep while you're here, that's all.' And suddenly

151

she was gone, pulling the door behind her, and he heard the rusty key grind in the lock.

'Goodbye, Kes,' she said from the other side. Then there was a faint whisper of her bare feet going away, and he was abandoned.

And the moonlight streamed on, breaking the sill of the open window like a dam. That was the way home, the only way he could go. He was alone again.

His head banged like an engine. He groaned aloud, burying his face in the pillow, which smelled of her, sweetly.

TEN

The news of Deborah's desertion was soon known (news always was) to Charlie Yandana; and it was he, lounging on the bench by my door in the early morning, who passed it on to me. He looked rather pleased, I noticed.

I remarked: 'You don't seem to like Kes.'

'You know anyone that like Kes?' he asked, with his reserved white grin.

'Only Byrnie.'

'Aw, Byrnie,' Charlie said. 'He kidding himself.'

I had to admit that this was probably true. But all my thought, at that time, was of Kestrel. What was he doing? What would he do? Charlie could not tell; and I was seized, while I thought of it, by an obscure unease, a dread, almost, as of something about to happen that might touch all of us. These fears are not rare with me, but I am nevertheless disturbed on that account. And so I couldn't rest until

I had seen for myself how and where and in what mood Kestrel was.

I went down the deserted road to the deserted hotel. The front door of the bar was closed, and not only closed but bolted, an unheard-of thing. My heavy knocking brought no response, although Kestrel's dog was wakened by it, and came round from the shade on the far side of the building to enquire into my business.

'Where could he go?' I remarked to the dog. And to find out I made my way to the back, and passed through the narrow alley beside the garage, into the blind-eyed and staring courtyard.

He was sitting in the kitchen. I could see him there, at the table, through the open door. The dog saw him too, and bounded ahead of me and pressed against his leg, ingratiatingly.

He looked up at me as I loomed in the doorframe. Those pale grey eyes of his were almost white; uncanny. He disturbed me, looking at me so neutrally, so incurious, as if I had been inanimate.

'I've heard the news,' I said.

He said nothing; just went on looking at me in that cool and (I suddenly realized) slightly ironic way. I came forward and sat myself down at the table.

'Well,' I said, at length, 'I don't suppose you were surprised.'

'No,' he said. 'It was coming.'

'What will you do?'

'Why should you care?'

He was looking down, bored by me, at the paper in

front of him, on which he was engaged in arithmetic of some kind, perhaps bookkeeping. I put my hard cracked hand over his, lying beside the paper.

'I'm sorry,' I said.

He looked up, surprised. Even softened, I fancy, for a moment. Because he said, without mockery: 'That's nice of you.'

'But I think Deborah was right.'

'You can think that, if you like.'

'You'll be lonely.'

'I'm not the sort of bloke,' he said, 'who gets lonely.'

'D'you think she'll never come back?'

'I wouldn't say never,' he said, meeting my gaze with sudden silver-eyed candour, 'but something's going to change before she does.'

'What?' I asked.

'It doesn't matter.'

'What has she said to you?'

'You want to know?' he asked, with his chin on his hand, regarding me. And when I nodded he began to tell me, at length and in detail, and I found myself plunged without warning into their life together, back to the time before the diviner appeared; into all the ebb and flow of their resentments and their exhilaration, into all that concerned them, up till the last parting on the previous night. And as I listened to him I began to have a good deal of pity for him, because he was the man he was, trapped in his selfhood as the flies in the bar were trapped in their small cages; but also I began to fear him, I began to hate him, and I could not explain to myself why, and I began to feel a measure of guilt on this account, since he was being so candid with me, and confiding in me, as if he trusted my judgement. I was afraid of him, and I could not meet his eyes, which were so unusually honest.

When he had finished, I brought myself to say that Deborah's revulsion of feeling might soon pass. But I couldn't believe it; certainly I couldn't hope it.

He looked at me with a spark of something like contempt, and picked up his pencil, and began to tap with it on the paper, making little dots.

'What will you do?' I asked, when this small sound in the silence became too trying.

'I'm going to give a party,' he said, with a faint bent smile.

'A party,' I said. 'In Tourmaline. Good Lord.'

'It's the right night for it, with the truck coming tomorrow.'

'And who will you ask?'

'Everyone. Including the camp.'

'This is some wild scheme you're hatching,' I said.

And he said: 'Maybe.'

A small flake of paint floated down from the ceiling, on to the table, between us. He broke it up, idly, with his pencil point.

'I'm scared of you,' I said, surprising myself as I said it. But it was true. There was a tightness in me, an internal trembling, that might soon communicate itself to my hands. And he would only smile, gouging the tabletop with his pencil. 'I don't understand you,' I said. He went on stabbing the soft pine surface. 'Stop it,' I said, taking the pencil from him, and standing, my hands on the table, bending over him, while he looked up at me with his thin and pale-eyed grin. 'There's something wrong. There's something wrong.'

'Sure,' he said. 'But what can you do?'

'Nothing.'

'Why don't you lock me up,' he said, softly. 'You're the Law.'

'Ah, for how long?'

He shrugged. And a few more scraps of paint descended, lying like snowflakes on his hair and on mine, while I stared at him, thinking: Something wrong. There's something wrong.

He began when the dark began. Every lamp and lantern the hotel had ever possessed was filled, and wicks were made, where necessary, out of old rags. Every door was open, every window glowed. All the bare bedrooms were lit up, with their horrors of carpeting dust, of flaking paint, of rust-red sagging bedsprings. God knows what he meant by it. But it was painful to me to come again, after so many years, into the room that had once been a kind of private lounge, and to see the dreadful armchairs puff clouds of dust as bodies flopped upon them, and the nests of dead insects in vases and smokers' stands, and the curtains gently disintegrating at the brush of a passing shoulder. Let me confess it, I am half in love with ruin. But it is hard, it is too hard to bear, without due warning.

Outside, by the war memorial, a bonfire was burning. Charlie Yandana and his brother Gentle Jesus had built it, and people came continually from the camp with roots and branches to feed it, and stood to watch, black and spidery against the blaze. The white store was sunrise-red in that light, and so was Tom, observing from his doorway. But Deborah and Mary were inside, in the green sitting-room, with the door locked.

'What this for?' Charlie Yandana asked, prowling barefoot in the empty dining room.

'It's a party,' Byrne said, with a bottle in his hand. 'Yippee. It's a party.'

He lifted the bottle to his mouth, and swigged, and coughed.

'Give me some of that,' Charlie said.

'Get some for yourself,' Byrne said. 'In the kitchen. Or the bar. Take a bottle. Take a few.'

'Give me that,' said Charlie. And he took it.

'You looking for a fight?'

'Yair,' said Charlie, 'I'm looking for a fight. There gunna be some fighting tonight, by Jesus.'

'You watch yourself.'

'You not gunna hurt nobody,' said Charlie, 'poor old Byrnie.'

He wandered away with the bottle, towards the bonfire. And Byrne went out to the kitchen for another.

In the lounge Kestrel lolled in a dust-impregnated chair.

'What's this for?' I asked him.

'That's what I'm wondering,' said Rock, with a bottle in his hand.

'Not for anything,' said Kestrel. 'Just a small party for my friends.'

'Why aren't you drinking?'

'I don't any more,' he said. 'My young cousin out there's a pretty solemn warning.'

'That's no reason,' I said.

'It runs in the family,' he assured me, 'like wooden legs. I've got to be careful.'

I was not deceived. 'You're trying to wreck Tourmaline. To start fights going.'

'There could be cheaper ways of doing it,' he said.

'Then why? What are you doing?'

'I'm saying goodbye to the licensed victualling trade,' he said. 'This is it, mates. There'll be no more grog in Tourmaline.'

Outside, by the fire, an argument had started already. A woman from the camp was shouting at another, the wife of Pete Macaroni or Bill the Dill. And then Byrne's guitar began, and his voice with it, singing:

> 'New Holland is a barren place,
> in it there grows no grain,
> nor any habitation
> wherein for to remain...'

'I don't get it,' Rock said. 'What's going on?'

'Nothing,' said Kestrel. 'Nothing at all.'

'And how will you live?'

'I'm a rich man. I'm the gaping mouth you all feed with gold.'

'Is this what Deborah wants?' I asked him, squarely.

'I don't know what she wants,' he said. 'And for the time being I don't care.'

'But the sugar canes are plenty
and the wine drops from the tree...'

'That I can't believe,' I said. And he twisted his mouth
at me, sardonically.

'The lowlands of New Holland
have torn my love from me.'

'I get the feeling,' Rock said, 'that I don't know what's
happening. And what are they doing out there?'

The windows shone red with the firelight outside, and
shadows moved across them occasionally.

'Celebrating,' Kestrel said, 'while they can. Why don't
you? She'll be a dry town tomorrow.'

Then Charlie Yandana began one of his dirges,
drowning out Byrne.

'I'll go,' I said, 'and see—what's happening.' Because his
presence, Kestrel's, was stifling me. I went out into the hall,
where the big front door, so seldom opened, was standing
wide, and the blaze by the obelisk luridly lit what little
there was to light: a leather sofa, a spidery table holding a
jardiniere, two coloured photographs of race-horses, slightly
damaged by insects. There was a crowd around the fire. Even
old Gloria was there, sitting quietly on the ground. Charlie
went wailing on, squatted beside the war memorial. And
Byrne, on a step of it, above him, had ceased to compete with
him, vocally, and was trying to accompany him on the guitar.
Everyone, as far as I could see, had a bottle, and some seemed
half drunk already, more because they wished to be than
because they had, at that early stage, consumed much liquor.

Tom was standing in his doorway, red with firelight. I went to him.

He looked rather solemn.

'You don't feel like joining in?' I asked him.

'What's he up to?' he wondered, abstracted.

'He says it's the last liquor we'll ever see in Tourmaline.'

'If I believed him,' Tom said, 'I might be in it.'

'But you don't trust him?'

'He couldn't lie straight in bed,' said Tom.

'He's changed,' I said. 'Changing. Something's going to happen.'

'You say that once a week,' Tom remarked, 'but nothing ever has.' He spoke absently, with no intent to offend me.

'I can't help,' I said, 'my fears. My intuitions. Something's ending. And I keep thinking of—out there.'

Deborah came to us, from the dim flamelit depths of the store. She asked: 'What's he doing, Pa?'

'We don't know,' Tom said. 'But he says he's going to close down the pub.'

'That'll hurt some people,' she said.

'Don't go out,' Tom said to her.

'I'm not going to. Mary and I are locking ourselves in.'

The firelight made a hemisphere, with the tip of the obelisk its zenith. I looked up at the other hemisphere that enclosed it. Deep, deep blue, like the darkest sea, strewn with white conflagrations. Below, there was silence for a time. Then Byrne began singing again.

'Come inside,' Tom said, moving away. So Deborah and I followed him, into the green sitting-room where Mary was, and we settled there, to wait for whatever

161

might happen. Not that we were in any great anxiety. But Tourmaline has a young heart, and a whole town can't get drunk without involving itself in a few scuffles. While we were sitting there we heard two heavy-footed men race around the house, and the one who was being pursued was laughing like a lunatic, or like a very small boy. 'I think it's Horse,' Mary said. 'He's been pushing someone over.' She pulled back the curtains, but they had gone by then. The fire seemed to grow brighter every minute, and in the Springs' yard the lavatory, of once-white corrugated iron, was striped rose and grey-blue with light and shadow. It was rather beautiful.

'Has Michael come?' Mary asked.

'No,' I said. 'I don't think he's likely to, either.'

'He's a puritan,' Tom said, amused. And Deborah looked unhappy suddenly.

Two hours went by. The noise level outside rose steadily, punctuated with bursts of singing and wild laughter; and then the guitar, very loud and twanging, began to play a dance, and hands began to clap, and someone (I think Charlie Yandana) broke in every now and again with a most accomplished yodel. It made me feel old and bored and superfluous, like a matronly chaperon at a Bacchanalia, if such a thing can be imagined; and it came to me all at once that I have never, in all my life, been anything else. What could be more wretched than to discover, in one's extreme age, that one has had no youth to remember? I see myself again as a boy; a long solemn face, obsessed with responsibilities never more than an illusion, wearing unreasoned habit like a straitjacket. I was a good lad, alas.

162

A tool, a dupe. What price have others paid for my arrogant simplicity?

'This will never end,' said Mary. 'I must go to bed.'

'So must I,' said Deborah, rising.

'It could go on for hours,' Tom said to me. 'Let's have another look.'

'Or days,' I said, following him. 'Like the old race meetings.' And saying that I thought of horses, with great sadness.

As we came into the firelit store an uproar rose in the road outside, and then abruptly died into two voices only, shouting at one another. Dicko's was one of them, I recognized, and the other, we found when we reached the door, was Harry Bogada's. They were preparing to fight. The cause, I gathered from the insults that were flying, was Dicko's wild-looking wife Analya, who had retreated to the hotel veranda and was watching from there, in a spirit of dark contempt, while the two men took up their postures of defiance. In the red light there was something ancient, pathetic, ludicrous, about those black shapes, those traditional words.

'We must stop this,' I said. Because I knew sides would be taken.

'I don't think you'd better try,' said Tom.

But I thought it my duty, and went forward. As I came into the light there were shouts. 'The Law! The Law!' they called. And there was laughter, too. I stopped, astonished.

Then Dicko hit Harry. And the fight was on.

I stepped towards them, quickly, to separate them. But I was seized from behind, my arms pinioned, so that

I couldn't move. And Horse Carson said in my ear, quite gently: 'Why don't you go to bed, you silly old bugger?'

Then I knew that I was old, and I could have wept.

Meanwhile, the fight ramified and became a riot. The Yandanas and the Bogadas made up one faction, and anyone else who could still stand joined the other. Horse released me, and leapt upon Gentle Jesus. Bill the Dill staggered into the fire, and staggered out again. The flames danced and danced, and from the other side of the obelisk came constant aimless chords of the guitar, twanged out by Byrne in a semi-stupor. A thrown bottle shattered above his head, and he cursed.

Across the fire, by the hotel, I saw Kestrel. I called to him: 'Can't you stop this?'

He laughed. I saw that, though I heard nothing. But he had a habit of laughing soundlessly.

I looked up, and saw the endless white conflagrations, that age cannot humiliate.

I looked down, and saw ageless Gloria, humped in the dust like an anthill.

And walking down the road, into the firelight, the diviner.

He came and stood beside me, with eyes like blue glass.

'Can you do anything?' I said. 'Can you?'

'What do you want me to do?' he asked, all taut and still.

'Stop this. Send them home. Because our unity—our esprit de corps——'

His bubbling laugh welled up, mystifying me. He was elated. He was watching Kestrel, who was watching him, across the fire, with the flame dancing in his pale eyes.

164

'Can you?' I pleaded again, in my helplessness and my humiliation.

And he said, quietly: 'I think so.' And suddenly he was among the flames, kicking away the burning wood, and leaping back, and then again attacking the fire, embers and brands scattering from his heavy boots. The fighting ceased. Kestrel jumped aside as a flaming stick struck him. The light rose and fell, like breathing.

Then he stopped. And he stood there, ringed with the dying fire, all blue and golden, but cold as ice, and silent.

'Michael!' That was Deborah calling, from behind Tom.

While he burned, in the fading light, all blue and golden.

I saw Kestrel turn and go into the hotel. And one by one the lamps went out, behind the painted windows.

The diviner stepped over his fence of fire. He stooped to help old Gloria to her feet. And we watched him go away, while the small flames died in the embers, and the old cold starlight took hold of everything.

In the middle of the street the blackened sticks still lay. Men sat in the dust, under the verandas of the store and the closed hotel. The afternoon light was severe, and many hid their eyes from it, with arms clasped round sharp knees.

I turned, coming down the road, and saw the diviner following. I waited for him. In the normal light he looked, once again, ordinary and prepossessing, except for those eyes, which were of a colour no one has seen before, and a little disturbing on that account.

I said: 'Good day,' and no more, not knowing how to mention the previous night. And nor did he, and nor did any of those about us.

Byrne was sprawled on the step of the war memorial, asleep, with a greasy hat over his eyes. We went and sat beside him, in the draining sunlight. He did not stir.

Ahead, the red road ran straight as a fence, through the boundless and stone-littered wilderness, towards the blue hills piled on the horizon like storm-clouds.

At last, another cloud showed. And the truck, in a puff of red dust, with a glint of metal, came crawling towards us.

We got up, all but Byrne. A murmur rose. 'The truck. The truck.' And Mary appeared at her doorway. But Kestrel's door was closed.

And the truck came on, with its yellow hand dangling beside the driver's door, and swept around the obelisk, and drew up before the hotel. The cab-door opened, and the small insect-driver descended, looking for Kestrel.

Then the front door of the hotel creaked back, and Kestrel called out: 'Come in a minute.' And the small man, wiping his hands on the seat of his trousers, speaking to no one, stepped through and vanished.

The diviner was staring, expressionless.

'Something's wrong,' I said.

Byrne slowly sat up, the hat falling from his head, and rubbed his eyes with black-nailed fists, sighing.

Four men were on the back of the truck, unloading. Rock shouted through the open doorway: 'What about the grog, Kes?'

'Leave it,' came Kestrel's voice. 'It's going back.'

166

'What are you doing in there? Want a hand?'

'We're right,' Kestrel called, coming nearer. Then the driver appeared, and behind him Kestrel, and between them a wooden chest with rope handles, whose weight made them stagger.

'You can help us get this aboard,' Kestrel said. And four men, straining, lifted the box on to the truck, while he stood back.

I was not watching the chest. I was watching Kestrel. He was dressed in neat khaki, and wore a most respectable hat.

The diviner was staring.

The men jumped down from the truck. The driver looked at the load and approved of it. He climbed up into the high cab behind the wheel. Then he opened the passenger door. And Kestrel, passing in front of the truck, over which the air shimmered like running water, climbed up beside him.

Byrne had been next to me, tense with suspicion. Suddenly he shouted: 'Kes!' and ran forward. He looked berserk. Kestrel had not yet slammed the door, and Byrne, with a single leap, had piled in on top of him.

The diviner called out something.

There was a struggle going on in the truck. Kestrel's hat was knocked off, and he was singing out for someone to remove Byrne. But he won, in the end, without help, and Byrne came tumbling down, grabbing at the door as he fell, and staggered over and lay flat, among the dust and the ashes.

The door slammed. And as the engine started, Kestrel leaned out, grinning, and shouted to the diviner: 'Look after Tourmaline for me.'

And the truck crept away; through the galah-feather dust, towards the far blue ranges, like storm-clouds on the horizon. The worn tyres left tracks sharp as new carving. The diviner was staring. We all were.

While Byrne, in the dust, cried: 'Bring back my ma, Kes. Kes, bring back my ma.'

—On that night I began to write my testament.

ELEVEN

The call of a bugle in the early morning. In the cool, in the blue dawn, ringing as if in great forests.

I got up from my bed, in the blue-lit room. I went out to the veranda, to the table beside the kitchen door, where an enamel basin stood; and pouring into this a little reddish water I washed myself, the small dawn breeze cool on my wet skin. It is for this I live nowadays, for the pleasures of my senses; a scent of leaves, a voice, a breeze on my dripping body.

The senses decay, alas; the world withdraws. The earth too, that with shortened breath and clenching scrotum I have so loved, the earth will fade and be drawn away, like pools to the sun. Dear God, let me fall still quick, let me fall responsive.

The bugle rang, on the wide cool heights of the air. The day of the dead began.

I dressed, in the blue light, and went out into the road. The town was all in shadow, but behind the two hills to the east the sky was fire-golden, and the church rose, burning. The lonely bugle call came again, from the end of the road, where Charlie Yandana stood with his head thrown back and the bright instrument glimmering.

Others were making their way towards him. I saw Jack Speed coming down from the mine, in company with Dave and the faithful Jimmy Bogada, who must have come in on the previous night. Rock came from his shack and fell in beside me as I passed, and looking back I saw Byrne and the diviner turning into the road from the track behind my gaol.

We stopped by the war memorial. Slowly the others gathered, from the shanties and from the camp, called by that ancient and haunting bugle-cry, whose sound to me is like the memory of a grief so old that all pain is gone from it and nothing remains but a kind of pleasure, a bitter-sweet reminder of vitality in which grief was possible. We have no ceremony, no celebration, but this.

Slowly they gathered. And Mary came to me, carrying a wreath of leaves she had made, as on every year. And as on every other year I went forward and laid it at the foot of the obelisk, the tip of which was receiving the first rays of the sun from over the small hills.

I turned to address them all, watching the light slide down their still bodies. I said what was true, that I had nothing new to say. 'We come every year to remember the dead, and there's not much more to add. Once it was said they died for us. But we've never truly known what they died for. Some for us, some for God, some for themselves. Most for no one, for nothing, not understanding, not even asking. Once it was taught that their death was somehow to our credit. We would come, in the name of the dead, to admire ourselves. That was a long time ago. Now all we understand is that we don't understand. But we come in humility, and in guilt, knowing that in some way we are all murderers, we are all cannibals, and the dead have been our victims. We come to acknowledge our guilt to the dead, because we have eaten their flesh and drunk their blood, and because their curse is on us, and the seed is dead in the ground and in the bodies of men and women, because of them. And in remembering them we remember also God, who lives and reigns in the galaxies outside us, and in the galaxies within us, and was and is our judge and accomplice, before and now and forever; and we ask him, in his good time, to revise our sentence.'

The old words came easily. But I felt them as new. All eyes were on me, but I did not think of myself, I did not imagine myself standing, pontifical, before the obelisk. I spoke as a voice from the stone; I felt myself to be the stone, the law and memory of Tourmaline. They were not my eyes that met Dave Speed's; and what his eyes saw was not me.

Again the bugle sounded, on the empty fire-flooded heights. And when it had trailed away we began to sing, raggedly and uncertainly, a hymn of which no one remembers the words, but which is nevertheless the only formal expression of our unity. And when that ended the bugle broke out again, wild with triumph this time, but dwindling to grief, and then again reviving, and sending its brave cry to wander through the immensity like a lone traveller in the desert, until struck down by weakness and sinking, without pause or tremor, to earth; and there, at last and utterly, dying away.

The diviner's hair burned in the sun. He was watching me, and the colour of his eyes seemed to me, suddenly, ugly; a deformity. He was studying me, and the others, like a scientist, cold as ice.

Afterwards I had breakfast with Tom and Mary. Deborah and Dave Speed were also there.

Deborah was like a ghost. She had never been more invisible. As for Dave, he seemed a little quieter every time he came into town. But signs of the old opinionated brawler would keep showing through.

'You did it pretty well,' he said to me, scarcely bothering to look at me as he made this restrained compliment.

'I'm practised,' I said, 'as you know.'

'Well, no one preaches a prettier sermon,' he said. 'And what would we want with a different one every year?'

It was not a talkative gathering in the kitchen. The dead were too much on our minds, and would be for some days. For we do not soon forget any event, and there is no occasion more solemn in our lives.

But Deborah asked, almost inaudibly: 'What's it all for? What's the use of it?'

'I hear Kestrel's voice,' I said; and may have sounded a little malicious, as I realized in a moment.

She looked angry, and demanded to know what the dead had to teach us.

'To stay alive,' said Tom.

172

I could not tell in what spirit this remark was made, and glanced at him, suspecting him of cynicism.

'To die,' Dave said, 'later on.'

'To treasure the living,' said Mary.

'But above all,' I said, 'to repent—isn't it? To atone.'

'Atone for what?' Dave wanted to know. 'To who?'

'To God, surely. For the crimes, the cruelty——'

'And save the dead from the consequences of their actions,' Tom said, softly. 'There's a plan for you.'

And Dave laughed.

'Is nothing sacred?' I burst out; in despair, because without bearings.

'Everything,' Tom said. 'Because nothing exists that isn't part of his body.'

'That we've wounded,' I said, 'that we've killed, perhaps. Tom, Tom, I think God will die.'

I remember the pain and guilt with which I said that, and the teapot in front of me: white enamel, chipped, showing steel-blue underneath.

'Dying's not serious,' Tom said. 'Everything's indestructible. If God can die, he'll die in glory. Watch out for the flowers on his grave.'

'Ah,' I said, 'the way you talk——'

'It's you that keeps throwing words around,' Dave said. 'Stone me, you pick up words like a bower-bird, and what a balls of a nest you make with them. Words are no good. Words are crap. Throw 'em away, and think.'

'Think of what?' I asked, or begged to know.

'There's no word for it,' Tom said. 'You can call it the nameless, if you need a name.'

When he spoke of it there was great strength and quietness in his face and body. And Dave was the same.

'So,' said Tom, 'we needn't talk about it again.' And he reached for the teapot, and as he moved whatever it was that had been holding the three of us together snapped, leaving me stranded. Only between Tom and Dave that impersonal understanding, wordlessly, endured.

'Then——' I began.

Deborah was looking at me, at all of us, with great eyes.

'If we talk about it,' Dave said, 'we'll talk crap. This is one of the laws of the universe.'

'But there are feelings,' I said, 'there are feelings. As if things might end. That's the frightening kind. But on the other hand——'

'Have some more tea,' said Tom.

I pushed my cup across. And went on, defying him: 'Something might appear. Like a track that's been walked over, year after year. Stones surface. The true bedrock gets laid bare.'

'This won't happen,' said Tom, from some distance. 'Not now, not ever.'

'But there are feelings——'

'Bugger your feelings,' said Dave. 'They're the wrong kind.'

And Tom said, more gently: 'Dangerous. You're dangerous. I wish to God you were the only one.'

Deborah got up and wandered out of the house, casually, as if to fetch something.

'I don't understand you,' I protested to them. 'What do

you mean? Can't you talk in words?' But they said nothing at all; more in sorrow than reproof.

Deborah went past my gaol, and on, until she came to the point where two paths diverged, one leading to the old huts, the other to the church.

She meant to go to the diviner's hut. But looking up the red hillside, glinting with sharp edges of broken rock, she saw Byrne coming down from the church. And so she sat down to wait for him, on a hot boulder.

He came with his pitted face dark and rapt, and did not see her at first.

'Byrnie,' she called.

Then he started, and turned aside towards her.

'Where have you been?' she asked him.

'Up at the church,' he said.

'Where's Michael?'

'Still up there.'

'What are you doing?'

'Nothing,' he said. 'Going to see Rocky, that's all.'

'Up there, I mean. You and Michael.'

Still dark and rapt: 'I don't know if I can tell you yet,' he said. 'Later on, maybe.'

'Is it water?'

'Something to do with it,' he said. 'I think.'

'He's been slow, hasn't he?'

'You don't understand him. You couldn't.'

'Will he mind if I go up there?'

'I don't know. Shouldn't think so.'

'You don't know much,' she said, 'do you?'

'It's the day,' he said. 'It's a bloody strange day. But go up there, if you want to. I'm going on down.'

'All right,' she said. And she sat there on the hot rock looking after him, until his drought-stricken figure had turned the corner of the gaol and gone from sight; and then got up and took the path to the church, glancing back now and again at the bleak and unpeopled panorama of Tourmaline that presented itself, and the infinite horizons.

The diviner was sitting on the ground outside the church, in the narrow shade of its front wall, with his knees drawn up and his head back against the stone, looking very high into the sky and seeing nothing. He did not hear her, or so she thought, as she came barefoot over the hard ground. She went to the corner of the church and leaned there, as though she meant to run away if he should see her. At length, idly, he turned his head.

They said nothing for a time. They had not spoken since the day she left Kestrel, and it was difficult. But he was very calm, very sure, by then.

'You didn't hear me, did you,' she said, to be friendly.

'I thought it was Gloria,' he said.

'Who?'

'Your grandmother. She is, isn't she?'

'Oh, Gloria. Yes, she is.'

'D'you have much to do with her?'

'No,' she said. 'She thinks of me as Mary's daughter. They all do, in the camp.'

'She's a fine old woman.'

'You mean, she's almost human,' Deborah said, with an edge.

'That's not what I meant,' he said, angry and shining. She shrugged.

He got up and came towards her. And she shrank back slightly.

'Things have changed,' he said. 'I thought it was me that was supposed to be scared of you. So you told me.'

'You've changed,' she said. Her bright, dark eyes were wary.

'What way?'

'You've got like Kes,' she said, in a low voice.

He was impassive. 'You reckon?'

'You've got like each other.'

'That's a bad thing, is it?'

'Don't,' she said. 'Don't be like him. I hate him.'

'Why should I care?'

'Do you *want* to be like him?'

'I want to be myself,' he said. 'To come true. And what you think I should be doesn't enter into it.'

'I never thought it did,' she said, sadly enough.

He was gazing into her eyes. Not naturally, not casually, but with some fixed intention, as if he meant to hypnotize her. She tried to look away. She was afraid of him, because of his strangeness, because his curious eyes were the colour, almost, of copper sulphate. But he reached out and held her by the shoulders. And when she still would not meet him, letting her head fall back and drawing away, he came closer and captured her face between his long hands, and went on staring into her.

'Don't,' she cried out. 'Let me go, Michael.'

'Why?' he asked, softly.

'I don't—I don't like you to touch me.'

'Why?'

'Because you—you're not——'

'What?'

'You're not—like other people.'

'This didn't worry you a while ago,' he said, with the rather dreadful insinuating gentleness he was beginning to acquire.

'Please, don't talk like that,' she begged him. 'I was wrong. I was wrong. Please, Michael, forget that.'

'I have to talk about it,' he said. 'To win you.'

'Ah, no!'

'To win you for God.'

She struggled again. But he held her fast.

'You're a harlot,' he said, still gentle.

'No!'

'How long were you with Kestrel?'

'Eight months,' she said. 'Michael——'

'Were you faithful to him?'

'Yes!'

'You're lying. Have you forgotten that day at my hut?'

'I was faithful to him!'

'Was he the first?'

'Yes!'

'You're lying. Don't try to look away.'

'There was only——'

'Who?'

'Oh God, we were kids——'

'Who?'

'Charlie.'

'And who else?'

'No one! No one!' She was weeping by this time.

'You're an animal,' he said.

'Oh, what are you doing?' she cried. 'Even Kes couldn't be so cruel. Not even to Byrnie.'

'Won't you admit it? Won't you confess? It's not too late to find God.'

'I've done nothing wrong!'

'You don't believe that.'

'Let me go.'

'Shall I tell you what's in your mind?'

'No! You don't know!'

'I'll tell you,' he said, more softly than ever. And standing there, holding her captive, between the corner of the church and the flowering oleander, he began to give her his interpretation of her thoughts and her desires. And what this was I cannot set down, because Deborah would never tell me, and I would not even if I could. It is enough to know that he poured into her ears such a stream of filth as she had never, and probably none of us has ever, heard, much of it dealing with her supposedly unquenchable lust for his, the diviner's, body. As he spoke he burned, in zeal and exaltation.

When he saw at last, that she had had enough, he let her slide down to her knees. And she lay, weakly sobbing, at his feet.

'Will you come to God?' he asked her.

She could not speak.

'Do you confess you've been a sinner?'

'Yes,' she whispered. 'Yes.'

179

'Will you come to God?'

'Yes.'

He towered above her, in the sunlight, all blue and golden. At the top of the path, beyond the oleander, Byrne and Rock were standing.

'Our sister's saved,' he proclaimed. And he stooped and lifted her to her feet, and dropped a chaste kiss on her forehead. While she stood, supported by him, like a baulk of timber, unable to speak or think, or even look about her.

I was wandering on the outskirts of the town, by the place where the Miners' Institute used to be. All has fallen down by now, only the Mess remains, and that is roofless, doorless, windowless, floorless. I ate there, often, when I was a young man, in the long room full of men and their talk, smelling of sweat and fly-spray. Now there are only the stone-and-plaster walls, dust-red, and the concrete piles that once supported floorboards, and among them rusting utensils of white enamel, basins and pannikins and jugs, the last signs of civilization, in this country, to disappear. By the empty front doorway was a painted board saying: MEAL HOURS. And underneath: *You are asked to be punctual.*

On the road to Lacey's Find, where a pub once stood, there was (is still, perhaps, if it is not buried) a billiard table; solitary in the desert, with a tall anthill growing through the centre of it.

I have played on it.

I remember when the Tourmaline Hotel was so crowded that men queued at the bar-windows for a drink.

It died in the night.

I stooped to pick up a sheet of paper in the shadow of the wall. *Dear Ned*, I read, through the smeared dust. *I don't know whether you want me to write to you or not, seeing you never wrote to me. I suppose there are lots of pretty girls in Tourmaline!!!??*

Died. Died in the night.

It was the day of the dead, remember. And my thoughts ran a great deal on such things. On such things as rusting pannikins, and the lone billiard table in the desert, at the centre of the curved world, commanding everything.

I let the paper drop. It was too sad. I watched it descend, making little back-and-forth swoops, as a falling leaf does. It returned to the spot where I found it.

I went away, past the big square mud-brick hospital where Bill the Dill and his wife live. There was a huge old armchair spilling its guts on the dirt veranda.

Because it was a shortcut to my house I pushed open the gate in the tin fence of Rock's garden and began to walk down the path. But someone called: 'What's the hurry?' And I turned and saw Jack and Rock squatting in the fence's shadow, not far from the gate, looking after me.

So I wandered back again, and sat down beside them, feeling the warm iron glow through my shirt.

In duty bound, I remarked: 'The garden doesn't look bad'; although I couldn't actually see anything of it, as the plants were hidden by brushwood shelters.

'It'll be better,' Rock said.

I asked: 'How?' And then, realising, said: 'Ah, the water.' To tell the truth, I was beginning to be bored with

181

the water. Hope deferred, in me, blunts the responses; and I was weary in any case. One rises early on the day of the dead. I folded my arms across my knees and put my head down.

They forgot me.

'My old man won't like it,' Jack said, to Rock.

'What's it to him?' Rock said. 'He don't live here.'

'Uh huh,' said Jack.

I heard him scratch the bristles on his jaw.

I wanted them to go on talking. Their quiet voices were very soothing. And alive. Voices of the living.

'What did he say to you?' Jack asked; rather tentatively.

'I couldn't tell you exactly,' Rock said. 'It's not what he says, it's how he says it.'

'And the way he looks.'

'Sure, that more than anything.'

'Like someone burning,' I murmured, into the crook of my arm. 'When he stood in the middle of the fire. Burning. And Kes ran away.'

For a while after that they said nothing, and I heard their boot-heels shifting in the ground, underlining the dense afternoon silence.

'Are you going to?' Jack said, at last, to Rock.

'I reckon. Try anything. It's a kind of duty.'

'But what he said——?'

'I believe it.'

'So do I,' Jack said, with a certain diffidence. 'It's the way he looks.'

I was half asleep, and asked in the shelter of my arms: 'Who is he? Does he say?'

'He'll tell you,' Rock said.

This afternoon hush, when a sound has ceased, presses down on one like tons of feathers.

'He'll be believed,' I said, 'whatever he says. Because of the way he looks.'

'Maybe,' said Rock, from far away.

I saw that I would soon be asleep if I stayed there, and got, rather stiffly, to my feet. And then the blood rushed up behind my eyes, making everything dark for a time, so that I had to lean against the warm fence and wait for the world to come back again.

'Are you all right?' Jack asked, beginning to rise to my assistance, as I could tell from the sound of his belt brushing against the corrugated iron.

'Yes,' I said. 'Yes.' And in fact it was all there, as before; but harsher, redder, harder on the eyes. The burning path through the garden. The church on its glittering hill.

'I'm a very old man,' I said.

This information could not surprise them as it did me.

'And no amount of water can change that.'

Rock sighed.

'I'll walk home with you,' Jack said, beside me.

Well, it was kind of him. And kind of him, too, to support me with his tough young arm, like a devoted grandson. He could not read my mind: in which a memory revived of savage kings, feeding their dead youth on the torn hearts of children.

TWELVE

In the morning I was sitting in my office, writing my testament that you now read, and a long shadow came knifing across the sunlit floor and across the page, and I looked up and saw the diviner, with a halo round his yellow hair. Charlie Yandana was behind him, and went and sat down on the bench beside the door; while he, the diviner, stood studying me, with his thumbs in his belt.

It was hard to see his face, with so much light behind him.

I got up, frowning into the brightness, and made some vague gesture of welcome. 'Come in,' I said. And he did, stirring golden dust-motes as he crossed the floor. He sat himself on the corner of the table, with one blue leg swinging. And I sat down again.

I remarked that it was some weeks since we had spoken.

'Two weeks,' he said, 'since Kestrel's orgy.'

'So, what have you been doing?'

'I haven't been idle.'

His eyes were lowered as he said this, but they smouldered in the crosslights, under the fair lashes. I had seen him like that before. It seemed years ago.

He had changed, and yet he had not. All his qualities, his contradictions, were the same; but now so intensified that they added up almost to another person. He was simpler, more innocent than ever; a solemn boy, indeed. But with this went such fierceness, such coldness of conviction, that the diviner we had first known looked pale by comparison, a faint shadow thrown in advance of the man who had now arrived. He seemed to me, now, rather dazzling; but dangerous, too, with all the ruthlessness of the obsessed.

'What does that mean?' I asked rather sharply.

He acted as if he had not heard me, and perhaps he had not.

I began to drum with my fingers on the table. This is a habit most characteristic of the old, I have observed; especially when consumed with impatience, or with dread, or when no one will notice them in their disquiet.

'Will Kestrel come back?' I asked him.

'I don't think so,' he said in a dream.

'But if he does?'

'We might have to take action.'

'What action? What is there?'

'We can decide that,' he said, 'if we see him.'

He went on meditating. And I went on drumming, glancing now and then from his profile to the knee and bare foot of Charlie Yandana, which showed around the doorframe.

'What do you want with me?' he forced me to ask.

He said nothing.

I slapped my palm on the table, and asked (too loudly, but I was unnerved by him): 'Who are you?'

'A voice,' he said, slightly smiling, with a kind of holy complacency. 'A voice in the wilderness.'

'Ah, this is old stuff.'

'Well, nothing's new under the sun.'

'Then what's *your* business?'

'To speak for God,' he said, softly. 'Because he spoke to me, in the wilderness. Now I'm his mouthpiece.'

This was said so matter-of-factly, with so little expectation of contradiction, that it should have been obvious to me that he had said it often before. But I was hearing it for the first time. And I was confounded.

When I could speak: 'In the wilderness?' I echoed.

'While I was dying,' he said.

'You were imagining, maybe——'

He laughed at me, young and genuine laughter.

'There are other things outside your experience,' he said, 'that also exist.'

'If you believe this,' I said, 'and I can't stop you——'

'Ah,' he said, laughing, 'you innocent.'

'If you believe it, what's that to me?'

'Everything,' he said; and looked at me so serenely, and at the same time so aggressively, as no one within the memory of those now living has dared to look at me, that I was abashed and let my eyes drop. For this reason, when

I think back to that interview what I remember most clearly is not his face, memorable as that was, but the corner of a not over-clean handkerchief or old rag of some kind hanging out of his trouser pocket, and his thin strong hand pressed flat on the table.

'Yes?' I said.

'Yes,' he said, or affirmed, with force and elation. 'This is your business, too.'

'How could it be?'

'You can be revived,' he said, 'like the land, like everything.'

'Is it water, then?'

'That, and a lot more.'

'Well, tell me,' I said. For he oppressed me, more than ever, and I wanted him to go.

'Did you feel,' he said, 'when you were speaking in front of the war memorial, did you feel—anything?'

'The dead,' I said, wearily. 'Their presence.'

'And God? No?'

'So faintly,' I said, 'like always. All guesses—guesses and longings.'

'With me,' he said, 'it's strength, it's certainty. And joy. I think that's the word for it.'

And indeed joy shone out of him, when I looked up.

'I've never meddled,' I said, 'with the convictions of people round me.'

'How could you?' he asked, cruelly. 'You've been empty, all your life. You haven't any convictions. Only guesses.'

To myself I said: 'I thought this day would never come.'

'What a respectable shack from the outside,' he said,

scorning me. 'And inside all empty, all derelict, like your gaol. The Law of Tourmaline. Weren't you ever anything more than this? Solid walls—empty inside? And in the dead of night a few guesses, a few longings, maybe, depending on what you had for supper.'

'What makes you so hard?' I burst out. 'This isn't the way we are in Tourmaline.'

'Tourmaline looks like it,' he said.

'I wish you'd never come,' I said, sincerely.

'Listen,' he said, bending over the table. 'There's work for you.'

I shook my head, dumbly. Ah, my age, my age is incalculable, my age is to be measured in terms of annual rings or sedimentary rocks, or by the changing atoms of unstable elements from which, aeons ago, I was created. And he had come to torment me.

'What Tourmaline is now,' he said, 'is what you made it. By your emptiness.'

'I had nothing to do,' I protested, 'with what happened out there—with those terrible things. They were others—all done by others——'

'And yet you were the Law here.'

'Someone had to be.'

'Why?' he asked.

'Because of the tradition—the esprit de corps——'

'You make me want to herk,' he said. 'But there's nothing personal in that.'

I begged him, trembling a little: 'Come to the point.'

And he said, leaning over me: 'I've come to fill your emptiness.'

188

'Ah, with what?' I asked. 'I can read holy books too.'

'You're innocent,' he said, smiling.

'Then I can enter the kingdom of heaven.'

'I've come,' he said, 'to tell you your duty. This is a duty you won't find in any of your old codes and manuals. And for the first time you'll be in touch with headquarters. These are no guesses now. This is certainty.'

With great tiredness I asked him: 'What is my duty?'

'You're to become a spring,' he said, 'an irrigation channel, if you like, to revive Tourmaline. This is what you should have been always; but you were empty as well as hollow, a poor shabby toy model of the Law. I'm here to wake you up, to tell you what you mean. You're to follow me.'

'What is the water,' I asked (all bearings lost), 'that's supposed to flow through me to Tourmaline?'

'Real water,' he said, 'in the ground. And rain as well. And the spirit of God, in and above all that. The spirit that works through me. It speaks through me now; and it'll work through my hands and my rod when I bring the water from the ground. But you're to become my follower, and through you I'm to channel the spirit to everyone. You're to become the Law again, more truly than you ever were. But I'm to have the real dominion.'

A voice like an incantation; a shaman's voice.

'"You are to",' I quoted him. '"I am to". These are God's words, I suppose?'

But he ignored my feeble defiance; indeed, had hardly listened.

He stood up, dismissing me. 'You're to come to the church,' he said, 'when the bell rings.'

'When?' I asked, in sudden unease. 'When?'

But he had gone away, without answering, stepping out into the light that outlined his head with gold and the edges of his clothes with icy blue.

I went to the door and looked after him. Gazed after him, half-doubting his reality.

'When that bell ring,' Charlie Yandana said, from the bench by the door, 'you come.'

'Why should I listen to him?' I asked; not of Charlie only, but of everything I could see, the sky, the dead tree, the gate.

'You better,' said Charlie.

(Who before has dared to menace me?)

'You better.'

The diviner went away down the road, his lean blue body a little stooped, like a horseman, and his gait slow, till he came to the store.

Burned sticks still lay on the ground around the war memorial. Dust was heaping on the doorsills of the hotel.

He went up the wooden step into the store, where Tom was sitting in contemplation.

Tom turned his head and looked at him; not smiling, not luminous, but cold and blank, a dead sun.

'You can guess why I've come,' said the diviner.

'Yes,' said Tom.

'Will you do what I say?'

'No,' said Tom.

'Why?'

'I don't happen to share your delusion.'

'You'll do nothing for Tourmaline?'

'For Tourmaline, yes. Not for you.'

'Then you'll be an enemy,' said the diviner, softly.

'It'll be an honour,' said Tom.

'Why are you against me?'

'Because you're dangerous. You're wrong. And it'll all begin again, all those terrible things.'

'If you speak against me, no one will believe you.'

'I've realized that.'

'Will you, then? Speak against me?'

'No,' said Tom. 'I won't do anything. The seed you're planting will grow and poison the air for a while; but I'll see it out, maybe.'

'So you'll come to the church?' the diviner said. 'For the sake of peace?'

'For the sake of peace,' said Tom; and he seemed as serene as ever. But all the light had gone out of him; a dead sun.

The sun burned to ashes behind the black church. I sat for half an hour in the blue light; too languid, and at the same time too unquiet, to get up and light the lamp. But one must eat, even when without appetite, and the time came to prepare myself a meal of some kind, to sit down at the kitchen table, in the yellow glow, and stoke the poor old machine, and wait.

There was now and again a movement in shadows outside the window, and on the church hill, under the turquoise sky, occasional flashes, like lightning.

Then the bell began. Not as it is when the wind is up,

but clear and purposeful, the way it has not sounded since I was a young man; beautiful and arrogant and summoning.

And the moving shadow outside, which had been Charlie Yandana, came up the step to the kitchen door and stood there watching me, all dark and shining.

'So I must come?' I said, facing him across the lamp.

'Yair,' he said, with two yellow lamps in his eyes.

I stood up, and bent over the smoked glass and blew out the flame. We were left with nothing but the light of the sky.

'Come on,' he said, turning and going down the step again. And I, like a tired dog, trailed after him, past my pale prison, and along the dim path that led up the hill to the church; from which came a red glow which was not sunset, but something more intermittent.

He walked too fast for me, and I called to him to slow down.

'Sorry,' he said, waiting. 'You old man. I forgetting.'

I caught him up, and looked at him, in the blue, blue light, bewildered by his intensity, his elation.

'What is it, Charlie?' I asked him. 'What can he mean to you, to make you so excited?'

His head was raised to the sky, to the black skeleton of the bell tower against it.

'He like Mongga,' he said, so quietly. 'I think that's who he is.'

'Mongga?' I tried to remember. 'Who is Mongga?'

'Mongga come from the west,' he said, 'and go through all this country. This his country, they reckon, and we Mongga's people—the people in the camp.'

'And what did he do?'

'He go from one place to another. He make a rock in one place, he make a hill in another place, or a cave, or something. Some places he make waterhole. At last he get very tired, and he think: 'I like to die now.' So he go deep down into the ground and he never come back again; and the water come rushing out of that hole he make when he go down in the ground, and that water make Lake Tourmaline. He make baby, too, spirit of children, in the waterholes and Lake Tourmaline and some places. He make everything for us, Mongga. But mostly water.'

'And *he* is Mongga,' I said, softly.

'I reckon,' Charlie said. But he said it rather curtly, as if this were a private matter that I could not and should not understand.

As the path grew steeper I fell behind, and he looked back impatiently. The church was hidden now by the angle of the hillside. The glow against the sky grew redder.

'What is it?' I asked him, panting a little, and waving my hand.

'Fire,' he said. And as he reached the top of the path he was suddenly all aglow with it. 'Look,' he called back. 'Here.'

I reached his side. The bell tolled on and on, louder with every step I took. In front of the church a great bonfire was burning, lighting up the whole hill, so that the flowers of the oleander smouldered with it, and the stone of the church glowed peach-coloured and warm. The door was open, and all the interior bright with the blaze. I saw that the pews had been removed and were standing outside, looking into the church, with the fire between them and the doorway.

I walked in a daze, seeing the skin of my arms grow red in the flamelight.

Dark figures were moving. Nearly everyone was there. I walked after Charlie, speaking to no one, greeted by no one, through the red light and into the church, the altar of which was bowered in green leaves, among which oleander flowers made occasional startling firebursts of scarlet. There was also (produced from God knows where) one of those statuettes of the Virgin in mouth-watering marzipan. The stone floor was clean swept. Silent people, white and coloured, were waiting there. I saw Byrne below the altar, with his guitar, and Deborah sitting against a wall, and Rock and Jack Speed, and in fact almost everyone: only the diviner and the Springs were missing.

'Sit down,' Charlie said, in a low voice. So I sat myself on the floor beside Deborah, who did not look at me, while he went to join Byrne.

All the while the bell went on clanging and clanging, till a pulse in my brain began to echo it.

I looked round, and saw that Tom and Mary had come, and were waiting in the shadow just inside the door.

Merging with the beat of the bell came chords of Byrne's guitar; at first very soft, but increasing in volume as time went on.

Then muted voices began to sing; so quiet, when they started, that I could not tell whose they were. But the song grew, and I saw that it was the camp people who were singing, led by Charlie and by old Gloria, and it was some kind of native lament, becoming louder and more plangent as, one by one, others joined in. Beside me, Deborah, to my surprise, took up the chant, singing no words, but singing, nevertheless, with force and emotion.

I wondered where the diviner could be. But the atmosphere was so strange and tense that to turn my head again and look for him would have seemed irreverent.

The bell pounded, pounded, pounded. It was intolerable. The singing grew louder, and more emotional. People began to clap, in corroboree fashion, in time to the crash of the bell and the great shattering chords of the guitar.

Byrne was crying. Deborah was crying. Charlie's head was back, and his smooth jarrah throat was swollen with singing.

I put my hands to my eyes. The bell tortured me, the guitar and the clapping and the throbbing voices tortured me. Everyone was singing. The noise was wild and tremendous.

I raised my head, and looked up, through the damaged roof, at the cold white stars. What are we doing, I thought; here, sweating together, in this small space, shouting together, shouting no words? What should this mean?

I looked down, from the height of the stars, and saw us united. All Tourmaline, all together; elbow by elbow, cheek by jowl, singing as one, shouting and weeping as one, praising God, beseeching God, wordless, passionate. I felt the power of our unity rise towards the stars like waves of heat from hot rock.

I began to sing, also, clapping my hands. I began to feel my oneness with them; with Deborah, on one side of me, with Rock, on the other. The strength of my love for them, for Deborah, for Rock, swelled my throat. Like them, I began to cry, I began to weep for sheer love, singing no words, singing of my passion. Love choked me: for Deborah, for Rock, for the light of the fire and the cold stars, for Byrne, for Charlie, for the clanging bell, for Tourmaline.

That was what he, the diviner, had done for us. There was never before this strength of unity, this power, this tremendous power. What was said, year after year, at the obelisk, on the day of the dead—what was said and felt there was only a shadow of this. It was he, it was our faith in him (faith which I, astoundingly, now found myself to share) that bound us, in love and passion, together.

Through my tears I saw the white stars. They too were singing. My brothers.

And yet, united as we were, we had never been so alone. Each on his small island, crying to be with the others, to be whole. The bell and the guitar and the meandering voices could not effect that reunion. There remained some act to be done, some act; and what could it be? Great pain, to be in love, and powerless.

I saw Charlie Yandana come to his feet, and in his hand I saw the bugle, brightly polished, gleaming in the red light. He stood before the altar, and brought up his arm, and raised his head, and his throat under the glittering bell was dark and shining. I saw his throat move. And the far forlorn call of the bugle broke out, widening the world, and the stars that had been so close swam away from us, and we sensed again the immensity of space, traced by frail emanations of our unity like radio waves.

The singing stopped, and the guitar. Only the bell went on, clanging and clanging. And heads began to turn, and mine among them, towards the doorway, where the black silhouette of the diviner stood, in a nimbus of fiery gold.

He walked on, where the aisle had been, through the breaking waves of our need and adoration. He turned at the altar, and the light washed over him, blue and golden. There was so much hope in the look of him.

I thought I should cry out, waiting for his voice.

He was not even looking at us; he was gazing back through the door, into the fire. And when he spoke at last, through the tolling bell, his voice was remote from us, though clear. 'God is very near,' he said. That was all.

There was a sort of sigh, a sort of cry, that our need wrung from us. Then the guitar began again, and a loud lingering call broke from the bugle, behind him. He started to move away, with his eyes on the fire. But our need would not let him go, there was suddenly a surge of bodies, of outstretched arms, touching him, embracing him, with kisses and tears; all of which he accepted unmoved, as if in a half-trance.

'He Mongga!' Charlie cried out, from the altar. And from everywhere murmurs and shouts came. 'Mongga! Mongga!' And an old strained voice in tears said: 'He is Christ.' These vaguely familiar tones I recognized (oh God) as mine.

He went on, his wake of worshippers behind him. I was among them. Who was not? Only Tom and Mary, in the shadow beside the door. I noticed, with half my mind, that

Mary was afraid, and Tom sombre, extinguished, like a dead sun.

Outside, under the cold stars, between the oleander and the fire, the diviner paused and turned back. The bell stopped, and Gentle Jesus Yandana, who had been pulling it, came out exhausted from the wooden tower. An enormous silence took hold of the planet.

'Go home now,' the diviner said. 'Don't follow me.' And he went away, losing all his light; head down, watching the faint track that led to his hut.

And we, deserted by him on the blazing hill—we found no anticlimax in this, that was the strange part. He was the focus, the awakener of all this feeling, but not its source. Nothing was left unfulfilled, nothing was the less for his going. Only, it hung in suspension for the time, it waited. The soul of Tourmaline, tingling and yearning; whispering: A beginning.

Below lay the township, with not a glimmer in it; only the pale shapes of its roofs in the starlight to show that it was still there. Lost, it looked, lying there, at the centre of the dark universe.

There we descended. Each alone, more alone than ever; but united too, as never before, solitary and united, like plants that propagate themselves from the same root, growing apart, but sharing always the same sap, the same food. He was the root and the juice of all of us; he, striding home at that moment, on the narrow dark path between abandoned shafts.

THIRTEEN

There was never, since I was young, such a morning as followed; never a breeze so cool, hissing through the stiff leaves of myall, or earth of so tender a colour. At my door, opening my lungs to the renewed air, a mad thought came to me: that the weather was changing.

I crossed the road and pushed at the gate in the garden fence. I think that for a moment I expected to find a transformation inside, great rectangles and trellises of vivid green; but it was as sad as ever, as drab and dusty, and the high fence kept off the inspiring breeze. Even so, the exaltation of the morning did not leave me; and Rock and Jack Speed, who were standing inside, were in the same frame of mind as I.

'Ah, what a day,' I said, pushing the gate, which scraped along the ground. 'I hope I die on a morning like this.'

'Why?' asked Jack, grinning. 'You want to spoil it for us?'

He has the kindest heart.

'I want to die happy,' I said. 'It might be important.'

'And hopeful,' Rock said. 'Well, you can't be happy without that, I guess.'

'I can,' Jack said. 'I have been.'

'So have I,' I said; thinking back, so many years, to a time when I was in love and not loved in return, and what joy there can be in an accidental touching of hands, or in the lines of a face turned away. Hope did not enter into that. 'But it takes resignation.'

Rock said: 'Maybe there's been too much resignation round here.'

'Something's been missing in us,' I agreed. 'But not now.'

'I'm alive,' Jack said. 'I'm glad it's happening now, before I start getting old.'

'Old?' I said. 'You're a baby, Jack.'

'That's the trouble, in this place. You get old without growing up.'

Rock said to me: 'Is he having a go at us, d'you reckon?'

And Jack thought he meant it, and started to protest. 'I don't mean you. But Byrnie and Deborah and me—we don't remember anything else.'

'I don't, either,' Rock said. 'Not really. It's like it always was, only more so.'

'Like it always was,' I echoed him. And they must have realized from my tone that it was a very grave admission I was making, and they looked at me with interest.

'This is a change of opinion,' said Rock.

'I know. That's what he's done for us.'

No need for them to ask, or me to say, who 'he' was.

'But the past,' Jack said, 'all you tell us——'

'The present's the same. Only more so.'

'I dunno,' Jack said, with his blue eyes earnest and disconcerted. 'If you take the past away, it makes the future kind of mysterious.'

With no self-pity: 'I may be the oldest man now living,' I said.

'You're looking younger today,' Rock said, courteously.

'And I can see now it was never much better. Only, I have this faint memory, more like a dream, of the old garden at home, among the figs and the oranges, with a swing under the olives and a little pool full of frogs and lilies, and those other lilies, the pink ones, that come for a few weeks, before the rain. That's the only complete happiness I can remember, if it *is* a memory and not a dream. And that's what he's always made me think of, from the time I first saw him.'

'I can only remember the dry stumps of orange trees,' Rock said. 'Over there, against the fence.'

'I can't remember anything,' Jack said, 'except what I can see all round.'

'We'll make a garden,' I said, 'for Jack.'

'Sure, we will,' said Rock. 'For Jack and Byrnie and Deborah.'

'Well,' said Jack, 'let me do the spadework.'

And I was suddenly touched almost to tears. By the beauty of the morning, for one thing; but more by a vision, an angel's eye view, of three men in rough clothes, one grey, one greying, one with hair like straw, alone and united in all that desolation, building, for one another, their faultless garden.

I went up the path to the church, full of love and agreeable melancholy, like a man revisiting scenes he has known with his absent and dearest one, knowing she will soon be back. On the hillside the breeze was cooler than ever. Years dropped from me as I trod the sharp-edged rocks.

The pews sat outside the church still, staring in. The bonfire had turned to a neat pile of ash, warm even then, retaining here and there the shapes of pieces of bark and slender twigs, though the wind was at work to shatter them. The morning sun, shining through gaps in the church roof, lit up the altar with its mass of foliage and wilting flowers.

I went in. It had that clean bitter tang of acacia leaves in the heat.

Inside the doorway old Gloria was sitting, and looked up at me with wary eyes.

'Hullo,' I said. 'You again.'

She was a woman of few words.

'Are you waiting for something?' I asked her.

'No,' she said.

'I thought he might be coming.'

'I dunno,' she said. 'I don't think he coming. He stop coming now.'

'Where does he stay all day?'

'In his house,' she said. 'Or sometime he walking about there' (waving her finger towards Lake Tourmaline and all the country behind it) 'looking for things.'

I said: 'So you watch him.'

'Yes,' she said. 'Always I watch him.'

'What does he do?'

'Nothing.'

I squatted on my heels in the bright rhombus of light at the doorway, facing her. 'Do you love him?'

'Yes,' she said, without surprise or hesitation.

'Is he Mongga?'

'I dunno. I think: maybe.'

'Charlie's sure of it.'

'Charlie di'n't see him,' she said, 'after he find that gold.'

'What was he doing?'

'He was here,' she said, 'cursing and praying. And making me pray for him. He was wild. I got scared.'

It was the first I had heard of it, and I said: 'Tell me.'

So she did, haltingly, groping for words while I watched her. An old dark woman with her hair tied in a rag, her legs bent under her as she sat, hands plucking now and again at folds in her worn skirt. Very grave, very circumspect; and, like her granddaughter, tending towards invisibility. Now that I had noticed her I began to wonder about her, and could come to no conclusion regarding the person behind the deepset eyes.

'Then I went away,' she said. 'But I could hear him. Praying, like, only it sound more like cursing.'

'But he came other days?'

'He come often. Sometimes he talk to me and some-times he don't. But I never seen him like that first time again.'

'He's changed,' I said.

'Still changing,' said Gloria. 'All the time.'

The dark luminosity of her eyes, meeting mine for a second, seemed to call me on to explore her, to establish our kinship in this matter. 'What does he mean to you?' I presumed to ask.

'I got,' she said, watching her fingers and the pleated cloth between them, 'no son.'

'Nor have I.' This deficiency I realized for the first time.

'And he,' she said, 'ah, full of light.'

Full of light. How clearly I saw him.

'And God don't talk to everybody. God don't talk to me. But to him—yes, I believe that. Because I never seen a man before that look so much like God been talking to him.'

Yes. Yes—burning.

'That's why I love him,' she said. 'And everybody love him, even young fellas like Charlie. Because he full of light, and like burning.'

I felt, suddenly, so close to that ancient woman (less ancient, certainly, than I) that it was like a seizure: a seizure of love.

I reached out, and took her hand. And she let me have it, and raised her deep eyes; which were no longer wary, but candid and trustful, like a bride's.

On the path from the church, descending, I met Deborah coming up.

She was beautiful, on that day. She was full of light: her eyes, her skin. The small wind tangled her hair, and the sun found glints of gold and copper in it.

204

'It's you,' she said, looking a little disappointed, but smiling all the same. 'I saw you from the store, on the hill there, but I didn't know who it was.'

'You thought it was him,' I said.

She admitted it. 'But it doesn't matter.'

'Your grandmother is up there, in the church. I've been talking to her.'

'She doesn't talk much,' said Deborah, 'does she?'

'She did today. About him.'

'She loves him,' Deborah said.

'So do you.'

She turned in the path to look back over Tourmaline, a movement like a dance-step, expressing energy and happiness. 'So I do,' she said, with a laugh which was connected with nothing but her own high spirits. 'Oh yes.'

'What does he mean to you?'

'I couldn't say,' she said. 'Not half of it. Not a quarter.'

'But some,' I said. 'Something.'

'Oh, being young. And starting—starting again. Joy: that's what he means.'

'Poor child,' I said. 'That's new to you.'

As I spoke she grew graver. But the light was still in her.

'Kes is gone,' she said. 'Cast out of me, like the devils in the Bible. He can't win again.'

'And yet he was right,' I said. 'He told you you'd fall in love.'

'He was wrong,' she said. 'When he said "love" he was talking...This love's something he's never heard of.'

'Do you hate him?'

'No,' she said. 'He's nothing. Nothing.'

'Poor Kes.'

'I think that too,' she said, 'now. But it doesn't matter. We'll never see him again.'

'You're sure, are you?'

'No one's ever come back.'

'No one's ever gone, in your lifetime.' I forgot Byrne's mother.

'Still,' she said, a bit bored with the subject, 'why should he be different?'

'Because he is different, and always has been.'

Immediately she brightened. 'Then he'll like it, and he'll stay there.' And she looked so happy and cool and young, scoring this small point, that I forgot what we were talking about in the pleasure of watching her. She looked virginal; and for a perilous moment I was on the edge of saying so.

I told her instead: 'You look reborn.'

And she laughed, the full lips pressing against her perfect teeth.

'It's like that,' she said. 'It is.'

'What could he have said, to do this for you?'

As soon as I had spoken I knew I was a fool, and wished the words back again. All the joy went out of her, and she would no longer look at me.

'I'm sorry,' I said. 'That was a stupid question—a prying question——'

'It's all right,' she said. 'It's all right. Anyone can know.'

'No, I don't want——'

'We're not to have secrets any more, he says. We're to confess everything.'

'To him, perhaps. But not to me.'

206

'To everyone,' she said. 'I'll tell you.'

And she did, looking away over Tourmaline while she spoke. She told of her two visits to him at his hut, and of his denunciation at the church. Her voice was made unsteady by her quick breathing.

It was hard for me, when she had finished, to think of anything to say. Although by that time my faith in him was complete, although I could see he had brought her happiness in the end, it was difficult not to feel that she had been brutally humiliated. And was still, underneath her happiness. Standing there, gazing away from me across country, she was not far from tears.

'Poor child,' I murmured, at a loss to comfort her. All other griefs can be softened by sympathy; but the humiliated suffer alone, unreachable. 'Poor child.'

'But it's all come right,' she said, turning back to me, and smiling, though with full eyes. 'It's all so happy. And hopeful.'

'Blessings on him,' I said. And: 'Amen,' she replied, with a shaky laugh that tried to make light of her passion. It did no such thing, of course.

From the other side of the war memorial, as I walked towards it, came sounds of Byrne's guitar. No voice today, but the instrument only: sometimes jaunty and twanging, sometimes fading into plaintive songs without chords. I came round to where he was, and sat beside him. He glanced at me, and nodded, but went on playing.

Kestrel's dog was lying at his feet. It was his dog now. I reached down and fondled the black ears.

'He'll bite you,' Byrne said. But nothing happened.

I looked sideways at him as he strummed away. A ruined face, dark and scarred; a face that had been through fire. A memory stirred in me of my grandfather, on a Sunday afternoon, reaching between the Bible and *Pilgrim's Progress* for his father's battered copy of *Paradise Lost* and dutifully reading aloud, while I, dutifully, listened, half-comprehending. 'Why did God spoil the look of him, granddad, if he was all that beautiful?' 'Because he was evil.' 'Then why did God make him, and why did he make him beautiful to start with? And will he get back to heaven in the end?'

No, said my grandfather. Not in the foreseeable future.

I grieved for Byrne as I grieved for Lucifer. Surely, under that distinguished ugliness, the marred beauty still showed.

'Why did God make you, Byrnie?'

'I dunno,' he said, still playing. 'You tell me.'

'I can't. Can *he*?'

'What do you think?'

'How can I tell? You know him better than I do.'

'Nobody knows him,' Byrne said.

'But he must have talked to you. He has to all the others. Even me.'

'He didn't need to. Not to me.'

'Because you believed in him, was it? From the beginning?'

'Yair,' said Byrne. 'Something like that.'

He listened to a fading chord, then he put the guitar down on the step beside him. Coming into contact with the stone it made a faint stir in the air, a reverberation divorced from its sound.

'Why?' I said. 'Why did you?'

The dog had sat up when he moved, and was shaking its ears. Byrne made a clucking sound from the side of his mouth. For a moment the dog looked at him, enquiringly. Then it leaped on him, and began to lick his face.

'Get down,' Byrne said, laughing. He sprawled on the step of the war memorial, clasping the dog to his chest.

'Why?' I persisted.

'He likes me fine,' Byrne said, with his face against the dog's coat. 'But if Kes comes back he'll leave me like a shot.'

'Why did you?'

'A dog's got to have a master. If the one he's had walks out on him he just has to go and look for another. So—I was lucky. I found one to take me on.'

For a moment I rebelled. Ah, I thought, let me hear no talk of humility, of abnegation. This self-disgust is spitting in the face of God.

But the heretical thought passed. He was right, after all. He was marred, and knew it.

'Poor Byrnie,' I murmured. 'Poor Deborah. Poor world.'

The dog broke loose and fled, and stood at some distance barking and growling at us in a ritualistic way. Byrne lay where he was, eyes closed against the sky.

'Poor Mike,' he said. 'Poor bloke. He doesn't know what he's up against.'

I mounted the step to the store, and stopped in the doorway, leaning there against the jamb, watching Tom.

209

He was reading something, and would not look up.

'Tom,' I said.

Then he did put aside his book, and scrutinized me for a slow half-minute.

'You too,' he said at last, sighing.

'Me too.'

I thought he looked older, and defeated in some way.

'Why?' he asked.

'Why not? What have you got against him, Tom?'

'It'd be hard to say,' he said.

'You must join us. If you could feel the power—the esprit de corps. A whole population with one idea——'

'A hundred minds with but a single thought,' said Tom, 'add up to but a single halfwit.'

'But he's inspired. Can you deny it?'

'Inspired, sure. But not by God. By you, by Tourmaline.'

'That could never happen.'

'You thought you needed him. You convinced him he was what was wanted. Well, good luck to you, Mr Frankenstein—it's a fine healthy boy.'

'You're angry,' I said.

He grinned. I hardly recognized him. He looked savage.

'Not angry,' he said. 'Just very, very hurt.'

'If we created him, what was he before he came here? Nothing?'

'He was having a fight with God,' Tom said. 'Just the two of them. Now he's dragged the whole of Tourmaline into it.'

'Is that bad?'

He looked at me with contempt. And it changed him, utterly.

He said: 'Haven't we had enough of these lunatics in the past?'

'Lunatics?' I said. 'Tom——'

'These black-and-white men,' he said, 'these poor holy hillbillies who can only think in terms of God and the devil.'

'He's not so simple.'

'No, he's not. But what about his disciples? What about you? Oh lord, I can see you in a few years, giving Jack hell for sleeping with a coloured woman and asking Byrnie how he's getting on with his masturbation problem. That'll give you an interest in life.'

I turned on him. 'I'm not like that!'

'Aren't you?' said Tom. 'Well, by heaven, you used to be.'

And I couldn't answer.

'You're right,' Tom said, 'I'm angry. I've talked to Deborah.'

'But she's happy,' I said.

'Happy!' Tom said. 'You see a healthy girl turned into a hunchback overnight, and you think she's happy?'

'But she loves him.'

'Isn't that nice?' said Tom. 'And hates herself. And he hates himself. But they both love God. It's as good as a bloody wedding. Ah, he's a bright boy, all right, to do all that in a quarter of an hour. It took Kes years to do the same to Byrnie, and he had no luck at all with Deborah.'

'How can you be so stupid?' I burst out. 'To compare *him* with Kestrel——'

'They're two sides of a coin,' Tom said. 'Shadows of one another. And how is it, anyway, that you've lived all

211

these years and not seen that a man who hates himself is the only kind of wild beast we have to watch for?'

'But don't we all? Hate ourselves? In different degrees.'

'We were given this sickness,' he said. 'By the incurables. Deborah can be cured, Byrnie can be cured. But not Kestrel, not Michael. There's nothing to be done for them, except ignore them.'

Suddenly I wanted to needle him, and I said: 'And me? Am I curable?'

'Poor old man,' he said, with a faint smile. 'Your memory's going. You've been cured once already.'

I think it was the smile that softened me, bringing back the old Tom, making him recognizable. 'Why are we arguing?' I said. 'We've never disagreed before. You've never been angry before. Silly, at our age.'

'Can I cure you?' he wondered, hopefully.

'You can try,' I said, to placate him.

And he did try. But so stumblingly, so clumsily, that it was difficult to attend. He unveiled his God to me, and his God had names like the nameless, the sum of all, the ground of being. He spoke of the unity of opposites, and of the overwhelming power of inaction. He talked of becoming a stream, to carve out canyons without ceasing always to yield; of being a tree to grow without thinking; of being a rock to be shaped by winds and tides. He said I must become empty in order to be filled, must unlearn everything, must accept the role of fool. And with curious, fumbling passion he told me of a gate leading into darkness, which was both a valley and a woman, the source and sap of life, the temple of revelation. At moments I thought I glimpsed, through

212

the inept words, something of his vision of fullness and peace; the power and the darkness. Then it was hidden again, obscured behind his battles with the language, and I understood nothing, nothing at all; and I let my mind wander away from him to the diviner, at the altar, brilliant by flamelight, praising a familiar God, through the voice of a ritual bell.

When Tom stopped speaking, I made no remark.

And he said, wearily: 'That was meaningless to you.'

I was candid, and said: 'Almost.'

'Words can't cope,' he said. And he added, rather bitterly: 'Your prophet knows how to cut the truth to fit the language. You don't get much truth, of course, but it's well-tailored.'

'He's not so simple,' I protested, for the second time.

'Ah, he is,' Tom said. 'Like the Chinaman who invented gunpowder. "Just a few rockets for granny's birthday," he told them. Boom!'

The diviner turned at the altar; burning.

The singing stopped. Only the bell went on, clanging and clanging.

Before the altar. The flame of him. The blaze of his yearning.

He leaned against the altar, his elbows on it. And the brightness then—all muscles and tendons taut. He looked at no one; he saw nothing, only the dancing flame outside the door.

'God is near,' he said.

A voice like a far bell.

213

'O God,' he said, 'O God, remember me. I work for your people. Remember me.'

The bell clashed on. He was crying. In the firelight his tears were like blood.

'Remember me, father.'

And the bell drowned in our cry. 'Remember me.'

Suddenly gold was in the air again, the gold of Michael's Reef, as it had come to be called. And out of this talk of gold a new expression of our unity, vaguely thought of, though never perhaps actually spoken of aloud, as the brotherhood.

It was a way, I suppose, of keeping alive by daylight the spirit of the firelit church. The idea emanated from the diviner; but he himself took no part in it. He had become a nocturnal creature, never seen by us except at those barbaric séances. Byrne was the only one who had to do with him in his less ecstatic moments, and even he was only tolerated for his usefulness as a messenger. Still, he was tolerated, and it was through him that Rock received instructions to form what a colder and more methodical mind than mine might call a co-operative society, for the exploitation of the reef. This brotherhood or society we were all, in the same message, ordered to join.

We met in the street around the war memorial, and no one was missing but Tom, Dave Speed and Jimmy Bogada—and, as expected, the diviner. Every remaining man in Tourmaline had come. I will call the roll. Because they are the names of the sons of Tourmaline, that I love to count, as a miser counts his hoard. Rock was there, with Jack Speed and Byrne as his lieutenants. Then I myself, Horse Carson, Dicko; Pete Macaroni and Bill the Dill; Charlie Yandana with his brother Gentle Jesus; Harry and Tim Bogada; Ben and Matt and Jake Murchison; and apart from the rest, and hardly with us except in the physical sense, old Gloria's even older brother Boniface, who was both deaf and blind. This was the heterogeneous mass that the flame of one man had welded into an entity.

What the diviner proposed was simple and uncommon: it was hard labour. We were to attack the reef and tear from it every pennyweight of gold it would yield to such methods as we should have to use. I remember feeling, as I listened to Rock, a faint unease, a sense of prevarication. What had become of the water we were promised? Surely that should have come first? But if anyone else thought this, he kept quiet about it.

And the gold, once won, and smelted by Jack Speed at the mine, was to be deposited with me. My capacious safe was to become the exchequer of Tourmaline, and I its chancellor.

I was somewhat moved by this honour. True, there was no other safe in the town but Kestrel's.

In the red light (it was late afternoon) all faces wore an expression that I can only describe as optimism not quite daring to declare itself. Undoubtedly there was a sense of beginning, of waiting for a birth. Not the mood of the church, but something more sober; the mood of men preparing to work with their muscles, a daylight mood. Something, in short (have I the right to say it?), sane.

Yet, in spite of all this hope and all this corporate feeling, which the gold had aroused, there was never a suggestion that the gold was ours. It was his; it was his gift to Tourmaline. And seeing how unquestioningly this was believed, I felt, once again, an obscure unease.

But if anyone shared it, he kept quiet.

I went past my gaol and up the hill. And I turned off the path, for once, before reaching the church, and took the track to the diviner's hut.

I knew he didn't want to see me, and would probably resent it. But I couldn't keep away. I wanted to look at him; to try to guess what he was. And I was not the only one, of course, to pester him in this way. No wonder he would go out at dawn and wander all day over the pink bed of the lake and through the bleak country beyond it, waiting for nightfall and for the firelight which was his wall against all intruders.

There was a scrubby tree outside the door of his hut, and beneath, a wooden box with an enamel basin on it. He was stooping over this, washing himself, or (more accurately) wiping himself with a damp brownish rag.

His blue shirt hung on the tree. I noticed a line of red dirt, that he probably didn't know about, on the skin of his back just above his belt, trapped in the faint down there. But more than that I noticed, as one couldn't help, the deep hollow scar behind his heart.

I said: 'Hullo,' apprehensively.

He turned so sharply that one would have thought I had caught him at something shameful. And my eyes were drawn then, naturally, to the other scar on his left breast.

He said: 'Oh, you,' with a trace of relief, I thought, but sounding annoyed nevertheless. And he reached out quickly for his shirt and began to put it on, in such a clumsy way that I realized he was using it to hide the scar from me.

And with a kind of dull misery I asked myself: But why the heart? Why not the head, if it was dying he meant?

'We've seen it,' I said; like a fool, thinking aloud.

'Seen what?' he asked, with his dreadful eyes on me. No one else in the world has ever had eyes of quite that colour.

'The wound. The scar. When you were sick. Everyone's seen it.'

'I was afraid of that,' he said.

'How could you do it?'

'It's my life,' he said.

'And robbed us of you. Robbed Tourmaline.'

He shrugged. He tried to grin. But his lips trembled.

'But you won't—again?'

He looked down at his hands, methodically tucking his shirt into his trousers, and would not answer.

'Ah, Michael——' I said, feeling so cold and wretched suddenly, in the hot sun. Because he had not meant to come to us at all. He had meant to die there, in the wilderness.

'Why should I justify myself to you?' he asked, in a low voice, not looking up.

'That's twice you've tried.'

218

'I'm getting more efficient,' he said, 'maybe.'

'Don't talk like that.'

'Don't tell me how to talk, old man.'

'But you're ours,' I tried to explain to him. 'Not your own, now. Ours. My poor boy——'

'I'm God's,' he said, simply and sullenly. 'Don't kid yourselves.'

'We saved you. We made you. And not for your use. For ours.'

'I'm God's,' he repeated. 'And my own.'

'I think you're selfish,' I said. It sounded pathetically feeble.

And he laughed, lifting his head and screwing up his eyes against the sun. And something in the look of him then was familiar. I had seen him somewhere, in a picture, perhaps; or perhaps I had dreamed of him. The laugh of a man with despair at the back of him; of a great hater whose hatred has outgrown its strength and died, leaving him empty. That was how he struck me: empty. And yet, still prepossessing.

'There's nothing I can say,' I realized.

And he agreed. 'There are limits.'

'You were right. It's your affair.'

'Now that you know,' he said, watching me intently, and seeming amused (although the humourlessness of him was actually aggressive), 'I suppose everyone will.'

'No,' I said. 'And no one listens to me, anyway.'

And he nodded. But he wasn't really concerned.

I looked at him, and I felt betrayed. So much health, and hope, and strength, in the look of him; there was nothing I would not have trusted him with, from his appearance.

One would have judged him, by his looks, invulnerable; one of those made without a doubt of themselves, without a second thought. And it was all deception. He was not sound. How could I think so, when he did not?

'What are you thinking about?' he wondered.

'Can't I help you?' I asked. But it was a question expecting no answer.

If there had been any consciousness of having failed, any regret, my sympathy might have reached him, might have found him human after all. But he had rendered himself almost without qualities; there was nothing to him but his ferocious pride, and his yearning. No creature on earth seemed worth his attention.

And still he kept his brightness. He confronted me like a locked chest, containing unheard-of things. If I could break into him, I thought. If I could. And I had a sudden ludicrous vision of myself, starving in the desert for want of a tin-opener.

Then the gold began to come in, like a harvest.

Weeks passed. Nights of fire and singing, under the voice of the bell. Days when the town looked uninhabited, for the gold drew everyone away. Even some of the women. Even Byrne's dog.

And the rapture held. Mary was converted. Only Tom openly persisted in his heresy. I let no one know of mine.

I felt the ranks close against us: against Tom and me, against old Boniface. Not that they wished to exclude us. But the sense of purpose that first woke in the church had strengthened in the field; this was no matter of singing, but of the employment of muscles and sinews for common gain, of sharing labour, of giving aid to whoever, wiping the sweat from his forehead, should say: 'Take over, will you?' and go off up the hill to the open cave there to rest. And we could take no part in that. We were the elders of the tribe, tolerated, but outside.

I said to Mary, looking about for Deborah: 'Don't tell me she's gone too?'

'She has,' Mary said.

The degradation of old men, feeling envy for what a girl can do.

'I'm surprised you don't go with her.'

'I'm younger than you,' she said, smiling, 'but no chicken, believe me.'

Yet she did go, once, plodding across the desolation in a broad straw hat.

Jack Speed worked at the mine, whistling. The gold flowed into my safe.

'The town's rich,' I realized with surprise.

I told this to Tom.

'What'll we buy with it?' he wondered. 'How about some priestly robes for Michael?'

'Don't be like that,' I said.

And he was ashamed of himself, and laughed. 'But fancy dress is all that's missing.'

Somehow I couldn't confide my doubts, or my knowledge. I let him think me a believer—or a dupe.

It was some consolation, anyway, to see so much happiness, so much beauty. Nothing is more becoming to the human face than hope.

Rock, in his garden, in the dusk, lifted his head, listening for the bell. I noticed his brown forehead, rough with knotted veins, and his brown eyes turned to the church, full of plans.

I saw Jimmy Bogada sitting on the step of the store, and I went away again. I knew Dave Speed was in there with Tom, and I couldn't face him.

I went back to my stone cell and waited, in the dying light. Then the bell began, with the first stars.

The diviner leaned against the altar, his elbows on it, as his custom was, and his head hanging, paying no attention to us. The firelight glinted in his yellow hair.

Over the weeks a kind of ritual had developed. There were actual songs now, or at least actual tunes, that Byrne and Charlie Yandana had put together. And the camp people would break out, from time to time, into their keening; so throbbing and so compelling that even I, knowing what I knew, could be moved by it to the point of joining in. Because the diviner, whom they praised, was only a symbol; a symbol for what I believed in, the force and the fire, the reaching unwavering spirit of man like a still flame. There were times, in the tumult of voices and instruments and tireless bell, under the white fire of the stars, when I felt, so surely, the presence of God, that my heart swelled. Then, for a while, I was one with Tourmaline, and the diviner was transfigured for me as he was for the brotherhood. He was our captain, our delegate, the son of Tourmaline, who had come to set flowing the holy waters locked in my rocky breast.

222

I write this, now, as coldly as I can. But you too will remember those nights of singing, the red fire on the hill, the white fires through the damaged roof, the clang of the bell. And the golden aureole, before the altar, of our delegate, our son, on whom we had settled everything.

On those nights I believed in him. Because he was no longer himself. On those nights we created him, dedicating him to the glory of God. If he had been an image, an anthem, a cathedral, he could not have been less his own.

'I have sinned,' said Deborah. She wept, for pure joy.

And old Gloria cried out: 'Make it rain, dear God. Dear God, dear God.'

The bell and the voices went on saying it. Dear God, dear God, dear God.

All that for years no voice had spoken. Holy waters, locked in a rocky breast.

The diviner raised his head. All sound stopped but the bell.

'Remember God,' he said.

He stared out towards the fire, while we remembered.

'God is peace,' he said. 'How did we know God was there? Because we were tired.'

Over his shoulder the red flowers glowed.

'A kid couldn't know God was there. A kid gets tired, and he goes to his mother or his father, and they know he's tired and they take charge of him. They know his limits. They won't let him break. But he grows up and he goes away. And he finds that no one knows any more what his breaking-point is, and no one cares very much. He goes walking round in all directions, trying to find the right way to go, and no one can tell him. And when he's ready to break, he thinks: "This isn't how life should be. This isn't what I was brought up to expect," he says. "Doesn't anyone care? Where's my father got to?" And that way he finds God.'

Byrne was rapt. There were tears of self-pity in his black eyes.

'This is what we pray. Take charge of my life, father. Because it's too hard—too hard. And I'm close to breaking.'

The diviner's voice was trembling a little, and his eyes were unfocused.

'He is peace. He is joy, too. He's every beauty you ever saw. Everything that ever made you go small and hard, in the heart or in the groin. Fire and stars and flowers and birds. And great lakes and streams of blue water.'

And everyone caught on the word, sighing. Water.

'There'll be water. There'll be a sacrament. A sacrament with water.'

His voice was rising. The firelit tears on his cheeks were like blood.

'Take charge of my life, father. I'm close to breaking.'

And the voices from all sides drowned the bell. 'Take charge. Take charge.'

Then suddenly the diviner was frozen, staring. There was something outside the door; not the fire, something he had not seen before. And all the voices died, and the questioning heads turned, one by one.

The black shape in the doorway came lurching forward into the church. It was Dave Speed. And he was laughing.

'What *is* all this crap?' asked Dave, showing as many teeth as he had. 'What's it in aid of?'

Somehow the bell only underlined the silence.

'You won't find no water,' Dave told the diviner. 'You? You ain't a diviner's bootlace. You're either a nut or a flicking con-man. Why don't you hop on the truck and go home?'

The diviner stayed where he was, leaning on the altar. He glittered like ice.

'Go to bed, you stupid bastards,' Dave said, addressing the congregation. 'Stone me, don't you feel silly? Get up off that floor before you all get piles.'

But the only one who moved was Jack. I saw his face as he went towards his father. He was suffering.

'Go home,' he said, taking Dave by the arm.

'I am,' said Dave. 'And you're coming with me.'

'No, I'm not,' Jack said, quietly, trying to drag him away.

'Here,' Dave said, breaking free. 'Don't try to push *me* around, young fella.'

Jack said, in a tense murmur: 'This is the house of God.'

'House of God?' said Dave. 'House of *crap*.'

Then Horse surged up on the other side of him, and fastened his mallee-root fists on Dave's arm. And between them, he and Jack hauled the old man away.

All this time the diviner had not moved; not even his head.

Outside, in front of the fire, Dave was still resisting. 'House of crap!' he was shouting. 'Tell that half-baked bloody crook to get out of town.'

Then he was suddenly quiet. Because Jack had hit him.

Jack came back, and went up towards the front of the

church, and stopped in front of the diviner. His young face was suffering.

And the diviner said nothing. Not even his expression changed. But we knew, all at once, that Jack had done well.

'God is near,' he said. 'Maybe nearer than ever.'

Then the camp people broke into one of their dirges, and the guitar began, and the clapping, and everyone was singing, and over everything, louder even than the bell, Charlie Yandana's shining bugle burst out in triumph. Frenzy. Fire and tumult. Because we had found an enemy.

Outside, between the fire and the oleander, under the cold stars, the diviner said: 'He was put up to this. It's nothing.'

And he went away, losing all his light.

And down below in the town, under his pale roof, Tom Spring was waiting for Mary. And who but Tom could have put Dave Speed up to anything?

'He's not,' Mary cried. 'He's not an enemy.' And no one contradicted her. But no one believed her, either.

FIFTEEN

I woke in the morning, in the blue pre-dawn, to the sound of the bell tolling as if it had never stopped. I thought it must be the tail-end of a dream I was hearing, or perhaps I had slept all day and it was twilight, and the evening celebrations were beginning up on the hill. But I got up and went to the window, and found bell and morning both real.

So it was reasonable to assume that the diviner, for some purpose, was summoning us. And I had begun to think it safer to do what the diviner said, for as long as conscience allowed.

It is, in any case, the best hour of the day, the only time when Tourmaline is beautiful. Washing on the cool veranda, a breeze on my wet skin, my youth came flooding back, and for a moment I was not in Tourmaline at all, but camped by some creek, under the river-gums, ready in a minute or two to go and look at the horses, and rouse my sleeping companions by the grey fire.

This spectre of my youth, like a phantom limb, stayed with me while I climbed the hill to the church.

Only Byrne was there, in the wooden tower, hauling on the bell. His tongue was sticking out with concentration. He had no time to speak.

I wandered to the edge of the hill that looks over Tourmaline. The eastern sky was like a ripening orange. The houses below were blue and metallic; the land sombre, shapeless. Then suddenly the sun was over the horizon, and the world took fire.

One could have warmed one's hands at the glow that burst from the red earth. This is something like a miracle. I can understand all peoples who have worshipped the sun, indeed I can. Perhaps I do so myself, at certain moments; but I have seen so much of it in Tourmaline.

In the street people were moving, looking up, shading their eyes, at the church; and at me, too, I suppose, silhouetted against the sky. In twos and threes they began to climb the hill.

I counted them. They were all there, all the brotherhood. I went over to the tower and shouted at Byrne: 'They're coming. Take a rest.'

So he came out, swinging his stiff arms.

'What's happening?' I asked him.

'I dunno,' he said. 'Mike'll tell you when he comes.'

I wondered, feeling uneasy, if it had something to do with Dave Speed.

'No,' said Byrne. 'Dave's gone, anyhow. Him and Jimmy went back to their camp.'

Meanwhile the brotherhood had assembled on the hilltop, and waited, all red-ochre-skinned in the new light.

'Here he is,' Rock said. And the diviner came towards us, swinging his rod.

Is this it? I wondered. But I said nothing. Because no one else had any doubt that it was.

'The time's come,' said the diviner, with burning hair. 'I want you all to see it.'

He turned and walked round the church to the north side of the hill, where it slopes down to the lake, having no doubt that he would be reverently followed (as he was, of course) and not troubling to look back. And he went on down, through the broken rocks.

The hill was steep, on that face. Trailing the procession, I feared for my heart.

He went on, across the pink bed of the lake. It was firm underfoot, crisp with salt. There is nothing on this planet more desolate. That huge emptiness, that in good seasons, long ago, I have seen so crowded with birds that they blacked the sun out, wheeling above the water.

He is going to the other shore, I realized. It looked so far. Could I walk so far? I was glad it was early and cool.

And he went on. Presently I forgot the distance, watching my companions. They followed so eagerly. They trusted so much. I saw that there was no way to protect them.

We came to the other shore. And still he went on, up a little rocky gully now, one of the affluents of the lake. We seemed to tramp for miles along this, but I was not really thinking about it by that time. I was thinking of Jack's garden, that he would never have, and of Deborah, and of Byrne.

Then everyone in front of me stopped; because, I saw, the diviner had stopped. He was hanging a little pill-bottle of water on the hook at the junction of his rod. Then he was holding the rod in his upturned palms, and moving forward, foot by foot, up the gully.

He was in a trance, it seemed; very tense. And so was everyone else. Even I. No one moved to follow him. We stood like anthills where he had halted us.

My mind drifted away from him, soothed by the silence. I thought about Tom and Mary, about Jack and Dave, about Deborah and Byrne and Kestrel. So many gulfs he was opening, for all his talk of unity.

Then, all around me, they were murmuring, they were breathing out heavy sighs of hope and trustfulness. Because the rod had dipped, and was straining against him, and went on bobbing and straining, while he stood in a trance, questioning it. And then it had mastered him, and was pointing straight downwards, and his thin hands had no control.

The brotherhood surged around him. He raised his head, and he looked limp; impotent.

'Well?' said Rock, stiff with suspense.

'Dig here,' the diviner said, wearily. 'You'll get it at one fifty feet.'

Then there were wild shouts, and they were slapping him on the back and embracing him, and Bill the Dill was singing out 'Freezer, boys' (meaning *Freezer Jolly Good*

Fellow), and Horse, as one would have expected, was trying to hoist him on to somebody's shoulders, or just lay hands on him. They were beside themselves, as the curious saying is; all but Byrne, who looked sad, and I, who repeated to myself: 'A hundred and fifty feet,' with scorn and disbelief.

The diviner broke away from them, impatiently. He stretched out his arm, holding the rod, and with all his strength he threw the rod from him. Cutting the air, it made a high thin sound like a whistling-duck.

Then he strode off down the gully.

I tried to go with him, but he went too fast. When I got to the edge of the lake he was well on his way across it.

The sun was still low; the world still kept its morning colours. The pink lake softly burned, like embers under a thin film of ash.

Very lonely he looked, in all that desolation; very spindly and frail. And dark, too. The only object in the whole glowing landscape that gave back no fight.

I wandered in the forlorn graveyard, thinking about him. Did I, in spite of our hope, want him to fail? Did I resent him? It was, after all, pretty clear that he had come to take my place, and I was not prepared to resign my charge to the first comer, without remark or question. I was the Law of Tourmaline. This was no light matter. And yet, for the sake of Tourmaline, I believed myself capable of humility.

The red ground glared all round me. Who would think it had ever been disturbed? I paused by the white marble headstone of Martin Murphy, aged 104 years. Once, in the dead of night, this venerable man was exhumed by a mob

231

of drunks who had been told there was gold in the coffin. That was long ago. It must have rained since then. The earth above him is smooth and hard as concrete.

All the history of Tourmaline is here. Like an archaeologist I can distinguish the different layers of our culture. White marble and iron railings mark the heyday. Then wooden crosses and other homemade memorials announce our slow decline. The white man's importance diminishes, the camp people take over. They have no time for grave-markers; instead they concentrate on borders. At the peak of their civilization they outline their mounds with neat ranks of porcelain jars. What huge numbers of small white jars there must have been in Tourmaline. Do we spring, perhaps, from a race which fed exclusively on a substance called Marmite, and preferred a coat of cold cream to clothing? But in time this culture gives way to another, based on the beer bottle; and so dwindles, through the sauce bottle and the baked bean tin, to the primitive simplicity of today, when all graves and graveyards are thought best forgotten.

Ah, the love of ruin is insidious. In the middle of regret, in the middle of complaint, it is growing on one. There is ease in dereliction. Action becomes irrelevant; there is no further to fall. Or if, by any chance, falling is possible, then only action can make it so; and action is therefore suspect, even frightening. And that I was frightened by the diviner I have not denied. I was not alone, I was with Tom in this.

But I did not will him to fail. I could not. Tourmaline is written on my heart. I would have taken water from any hand.

How touching it is, the earliest tombstone in Tourmaline. It is of rough grey cement, and the inscription has been scraped into it with a pocket knife before it hardened. *Kenneth Macarthur*, it says. *Struck by lightning. Aged 22 years. Erected by his mates.*

I did not will him to fail. No. I went so far, in the half-thinking part of my mind, as to pray for him. I willed the water to rise, and he himself to become all that he seemed to claim to be; all that he looked, all that Tourmaline believed him.

Because, even when my disbelief was strongest, he could disarm me. Suddenly, turning to speak to someone else, I would catch sight of him. And the brightness then, the force, seemed beyond resisting; and my mind would go back, through years like buried roads, to the kingfisher-flash by the creek, and the frail pink lilies, breaking the baked ground in my father's garden.

From behind the church it was possible to see across the lake to the mouth of the gully where the digging was going on. And those of us who were not engaged in it would go up there in the evenings to watch the diggers come home.

Deborah was always there, and sometimes Mary was with her. Their faith was uncritical and complete. And the other women, too, the coloured wives and old Gloria, could not have been moved to doubt by anything less than a divine revelation.

So I, who came every day, and Tom, who came once, did not talk about it. But our disbelief gave the whole affair, for us, a taste of bitter comedy.

The diviner did not speak, either. He came not only in the evening but in the morning too, standing apart, reviewing his faithful labourers down on the lake there like a general.

His hand had been forced. And did he believe? we wondered. I couldn't tell. And nor could Tom, or so he said.

And the excitement grew; and was at its height on that afternoon when I stood with Deborah and the diviner and saw the men coming back across the lake two hours before they were due to knock off.

They were bringing their tools with them, I noticed. And Deborah noticed it, too, and called out: 'They've done it! It's finished.'

I watched the dark figures coming across the lake. Finished, indeed.

They reached the foot of the hill and began to climb up to us. There were clinks of steel against stone, but no voices.

Then Rock appeared in front of us. And the others, straggling, massed behind him.

I looked at the diviner as he faced up to him. And something about that bitter resignation, that half-scornful defeat, struck my policeman's eye as familiar; and the conviction came into my policeman's head, and never left it, that he had been, somewhere, a criminal of quite extra-ordinary distinction.

There must be, on the moon, such silences as we listened to then; but rarely, I think, on our planet.

At last the diviner said, hardly parting his lips: 'Well? Tell us.'

'We gave it the benefit of the doubt,' Rock said, 'and

quite a few feet. But no good. It's a dry hole, and it couldn't have been anything else.'

He spoke quietly, even with deference. But everything was changed. The faces behind him were saying they had been deluded.

'Will you keep trying?' Rock asked. He was hoarse with dust.

'No,' said the diviner; so still, it seemed he might never move again. 'Ah no, Rocky.'

'Anyone might pick a few dry ones. Especially here.'

'Not me,' said the diviner. 'Not me. It's gone.'

And all the faces were accusing him. The picks and the shovels, bright with work, were glinting.

He turned away, raising his hands to his eyes. And he cried out, in a voice that didn't seem to be the voice of anyone we knew: 'It was there! The water was there. God's betrayed me.'

One last flicker of his flame before it died. Then all was over. He was nothing.

SIXTEEN

Life goes on; as I have often, in my long life, had cause to remind myself. One sleeps and feeds. And, once a month, the truck comes.

First of all the dust of it, very far, against the blue ranges. Then the glint of metal. And at last the thing itself, sweeping round the war memorial to pull up by the pub veranda.

We were all there, as usual. Only the diviner was missing, and had not been seen (except by Byrne) since the day God let him down.

As the truck came, we saw that the back of it had grown a canopy covered with a green tarpaulin. And there was a passenger with the driver.

No one said anything. But you could feel the dread.

When the truck stopped, Kestrel got out and went to

his front door and opened it. And he stood there, holding it open, while three men climbed out from beneath the tarpaulin and went past him into the hotel.

They walked quickly, not looking round. But I was apart from the others, and caught a glimpse of one of them. He had no nose or mouth; only teeth.

I tried to pray for him. And for us.

When they had passed, Kestrel closed the door. And he turned and walked back towards us, so that for the first time we could see him clearly. He came and leaned against the mudguard of the truck. Behind and above him the air shimmered like running water.

He was looking at Deborah, and then at Byrne. And they were staring at him; all bearings lost.

His respectable clothes were less respectable, and his face had changed. A mask it had always been, but a mask now with something new behind it. He had caught fire.

'So you got back,' said Rock, like a vague old man.

'It had to happen some day,' said Kestrel. His voice was somehow altered, and it struck me that all that uncertainty, all that baffled energy that used to sound in it was gone, that he knew now what he was, and would never again be angry or bewildered or in any way at a loss. He was a whole thing, and invulnerable.

I felt the eyes of Tourmaline measuring him, measuring his force. I felt the need that the diviner had wakened and failed to satisfy cry out to him. And the new power in him, his unselfdoubting and not unkindly fire, gave a calm answer.

He said: 'Will some of you blokes unload the truck? You'll find a lot of stuff there besides the stores: tools and bits of machinery and so on. Dump it under the veranda. The jokers I brought with me are going to do a spot of divining.'

There was no sneer in this. He had changed.

The driver had not left the truck, and showed no intention of doing so. He seemed to contemplate the steering wheel like a sacred object, and did not look out as Rock and Horse and the others went by and climbed up under the canopy.

And Kestrel leaned on the mudguard, easily.

We gathered towards him, Deborah and Byrne and I. Deborah would say nothing. But she couldn't seem to look away.

'Well,' said Kestrel, 'is he still here, the other bloke?'

'He's still here,' said Byrne.

'And there's no water,' I said. 'He's tried.'

'Poor bastard,' said Kestrel. 'Did that surprise you?'

Neither Byrne nor Deborah would answer.

'We believed in him,' I said. 'Most of us. And maybe we would still, if he seemed to believe in himself.'

'If you see him,' Kestrel said, 'tell him I'm sorry.'

'Why? What have you done to him?'

'Sorry for what he's done to himself.'

All the while metallic clankings were coming from the veranda, behind the truck.

'So,' I said, 'you're going to be our diviner now.'

And he grinned. So serenely and absently that it didn't look like him, somehow.

'That's the theory,' he said.

He pushed himself off the mudguard, and he asked, beginning to move: 'Coming back to the pub, Byrnie?'

'I don't know,' Byrne said, wavering.

'Well, your room's there, if you want it.'

And he went away, behind the truck, where we couldn't see him, and was talking to the driver for some time, while we stood in the hot sun, thinking about him. And when at last the truck started and moved off he was gone, and the front door was closed.

Deborah sighed, and turned, and wandered across to the store, looking tired.

The group discussing the mysterious gear under the veranda broke up, and began carting Tom's stuff over the road.

'It's hot,' I said.

'It always is,' said Byrne.

'I'm going home.'

'I'll come with you,' Byrne said, turning to call his dog. But it wasn't his dog any more, and had gone.

So we went up the road to my house, the dust-cloud of the receding truck ahead of us, and the village square (as I suppose one could call it) sun-struck and empty behind.

Presently Deborah came out again and crossed the road, treading down the raised tyremarks in the dust. She pushed open the front door of the hotel and went in.

Kestrel was waiting for her, sitting on the battered leather sofa in the hall. He stood up. It was dim in there, when she had closed the door. Their dark skins looked cold.

They watched one another, a long time.

'Is this for keeps?' he asked, at last. Very gently, for him.

She came nearer. She walked into his arms, and they closed around her.

'Ah, Deb,' he said, into her hair. 'Don't go again.'

'No,' she said, with her mouth against his throat.

'Why did you go? Why did you come back?'

'I'm going to have a baby,' she said.

He stared over her head, stroking her hair. He whispered: 'Mine?'

'Of course.'

'Ah, Deb,' he said, clutching her, stroking her. 'Ah, Deb.' And she suddenly laughed, for pure joy. She could not see his face, with no blood in it.

Byrne did me the honour of coming to sing on the bench outside my door.

I stepped out to listen to him. I studied the blighted face bent over the guitar.

When he had finished, I said: 'Poor Byrnie,' to myself. And he looked up, grinning, showing his rather narrow teeth.

'Why?'

'Because—you had so much faith in him.'

'No,' he said. 'I never believed he'd do it.'

'Then why,' I asked, bewildered, 'why follow him?'

And Byrne said, plinking away, aimlessly: 'He was there. That's all.'

The breeze hissed across country. The sun went down. No bell. No fire.

The diviner kept to his hut, up there on the black hillside.

The strangers were shut up in the hotel, seen by no one.

At the mine Jack Speed lay alone in his tall room.

In the shack behind the garden Rock washed his shirt, in dishwater.

Tom's cat, on the step of the store, slapped the face of Kestrel's dog, and fled.

While the people at the camp mourned; keening. Raising their eyes to the cold white stars, that promise nothing.

On the war memorial, with a hurricane lantern beside him, Byrne was singing. He had been there for hours. The front windows of the hotel and the store were dark. From my front door, looking out into the darkness, wondering what the wind was going to do, I could hear his voice drifting up the road.

> 'Tourmaline!
> Red wind, red sun.
> I thought I'd never come
> to Tourmaline.'

Then there would be silence; and I imagined him, vacant, his guitar on his knees and his head back against the obelisk, staring at the stars. Making up a new song, it could be; for he is the poet of Tourmaline.

I went to bed, closing all doors and windows against the dust. Even then, I could hear outside the steady hiss of the wind, beating across country through the stiff leaves.

Deborah came to the hotel door with a lamp, and called: 'Byrnie, are you going to keep that up all night?'

'It's like old times,' he said. But she didn't hear, and thought he had decided to ignore her, so she went away.

241

He went on playing, not singing, just fingering over old tunes. It was the diviner's music he was playing.

And the diviner, as if summoned, suddenly loomed up out of the darkness, breaking into the small sphere of light.

The yellow glow turned his terrible eyes green. He looked sick; haggard. And furtive, too, like someone expecting to be set upon.

'I thought you weren't coming here any more,' Byrne said, watching his own moving fingers.

'I don't know why you thought that,' said the diviner.

'There's no one awake.'

'I can tell the time.'

'Fine,' said Byrne, with a shrug.

The diviner burst out, in a rage: 'Look at me when you talk to me. What's wrong with you? Am I such a miserable sight you can't stand it?'

'I never was much good at looking people in the eye,' Byrne confessed. But he lifted his ruined face, and did his best.

'Dear God, you're ugly,' the diviner remarked to himself. 'It isn't fair.'

He sat down beside Byrne and looked up at the stars.

'Getting windy,' Byrne said.

The diviner said: 'Uh-huh.'

'Could be a dust storm.'

'Who cares?'

They listened to the wind for a while, and the guitar.

'Where's Deborah?' the diviner asked, after a time.

'Give you one guess.'

'Ah, the harlot.'

'It's her husband, mate. Fair go.'

'What does he say?'

'What does he say about what?'

'About me?'

'He says he's sorry for you.'

The diviner laughed, making deep creases in his unshaven cheeks.

'You've got a funny sense of humour,' Byrne said.

'I've got no sense of humour at all,' said the diviner.

He sat with the lantern between his feet, his head bent over it. The spikes of his dishevelled hair shone yellow at the points. The bones of his long hands shone too, gripping his sharp blue knees.

There was nothing to him: only his ferocious pride, and his yearning.

Byrne played on. He knew it was no use to talk, at that stage. The diviner was not interested in his opinions, or his sympathy. He didn't believe in Byrne's existence. For him, the world was a desert island, and it was up to him to make what he could of it.

So he brooded, over his lantern, like a sullen castaway seeking his future in the fire.

Dust began to blow around them.

'I did my best,' the diviner said. 'No one can say otherwise.'

'Sure,' said Byrne. 'No one does, either.'

'Why did I wake up this morning?' the diviner wondered. 'It wasn't fair.'

'Why don't you go and sleep now?'

'Never seen it so dark. So dark.'

'Take the lantern,' Byrne said.

The diviner held out his hands, warming them over the heat rising from the small flame. 'Cold, too,' he said. He was shivering.

'Are you crook?' Byrne asked. 'You don't look too good.'

The diviner looked round at his spoiled face, and looked down again. 'I won't say it,' he decided.

'Ah, quit taking it out on the dog.'

'Do you care?' said the diviner, surprised by a new thought.

'What about?'

'The way you look.'

'No, I don't care,' said Byrne, with a happy laugh. 'Far as anyone knows, I'm the ugliest bloke in the world. It's an honour.'

'I couldn't live,' said the diviner.

'What do you want me to do? Shoot myself?'

'No,' said the diviner. 'Not you. They'd only call you a bloody nuisance.'

Byrne kept on strumming. 'Anyone ever tell you you were a bastard?' he enquired.

But the diviner was turned off, as it were; not receiving any further messages.

He stood up, shivering in the wind, which tossed the shining points of his hair.

'You going?' Byrne asked, looking up at him.

'Yair,' he said, distantly. 'Going home.'

'Take the light.'

'I don't need it.'

'You'll go down a shaft. Looks like I'll have to come with you.'

'I'm not going that way,' the diviner said.

'You flying or something?'

'I'm not going to the hut,' the diviner said. 'I'm going home.'

And Byrne stared up at him, out of a dark face pitted with shadows.

'You'll never make it,' he said. 'Mike——'

'Home,' said the diviner, in a dream.

'Don't be stupid. You'll die.'

'Give me one reason why not,' said the diviner; not speaking to Byrne, as it appeared.

'Yair, I will,' Byrne said, in stress and pain.

'Well, what is it?'

'Ah no. You won't call it a reason.'

'Why shouldn't I go?' asked the diviner, smiling at the dark horizon.

'Because—ah no.'

'Why?'

'Let me help you,' Byrne pleaded.

'Why?'

'Because I reckon I love you, mate,' Byrne whispered. And he waited, with his terrible secret (he thought it a secret) at last confessed, to be struck by lightning.

'Oh God,' said the diviner, laughing. 'Oh God.'

'I haven't sinned,' Byrne said. 'I was damned without that.'

And the diviner went on laughing.

'Stay here,' Byrne said, from the depths. 'Stay here, Mike.'

'What,' said the diviner, 'to be equal with you? God forbid.'

And he went away, towards the leaning fence that marks the end of the road. Dust blew back from where his thick boots fell.

'Mike,' Byrne called. He dropped his guitar and went after him.

But the diviner broke into a sprint, and leaped the trailing barbed wire of the fence, and ran away laughing, into the gathering wind.

SEVENTEEN

The wind had got up, and was moaning in all the houses, through the spaces where the iron walls meet the roof. The country lay wrapped in dust like a light red mist.

Kestrel crossed the road, head lowered, and went to the door of the store, which was closed. When he opened it, the wind tore it away from him and sent it crashing against a table inside. A nest of billy cans came clattering down.

'Mind!' Mary called, appearing from the kitchen. 'Oh, the dust.'

Tom was sitting in front of the shop window, staring out. 'I thought you'd come, sooner or later,' he said, not looking round.

'Hand of friendship,' Kestrel said. 'After all, we're related.'

The dry wind whistled among the rafters.

'So you're the diviner now,' Tom said. 'I might have seen it coming.'

'Someone had to take charge.'

'Had to?'

'Was bound to.'

'Oh, sure. He left a gap, didn't he? And the organization was there.'

'What will you do, Kes?' Mary was wondering.

'Carry on where he left off.'

'And the church?'

'The same. It can survive without him.'

'And you'll be high priest,' said Tom, contemptuously.

'Someone will. That—power—is worth having.'

'That "power",' said Tom.

'Will you join us, Tom?'

'No,' said Tom. 'I'm an old man. Let me sleep.'

'You're the only weak link.'

'And proud of it,' said Tom. 'Leave me to die in peace.'

'And you, Mary?'

'Yes,' she said, looking at Tom, hesitantly. 'I will.'

'That's good to hear,' Kestrel said. 'That's all I wanted.' And he turned, lifting his hand to the door.

'Kes,' said Tom, still intent on the whirling dust.

'What?'

'Honour the single soul.'

'I think in thousands,' Kestrel said, 'and tens of thousands.'

A flurry of dust ran across the room as he opened the door, and then quickly subsided.

The dust flowed by the windows like turbid water. At midday, sitting writing at my table, I had all the lamps alight.

248

Then the door burst open, and dust showered on the page in front of me. Kestrel was there, and Byrne behind him, looking ownerless, pushing the door to with his back.

It was some time before the flames of the lamps calmed down.

'So you've come,' I said, with resignation.

'I certainly haven't surprised anyone,' said Kestrel.

'No.'

'What do you say?'

'I haven't much choice, have I?'

'No,' he said. 'Not much.'

'You want the gold?'

'No,' he said, surprised. 'You can be the banker. It's Tourmaline's gold. I'm not claiming it.'

'But you are, of course,' I perceived. 'And everything else as well. All your eggs in one basket, called Tourmaline.'

He grinned. 'That's one way of putting it.'

The dust was leaking in under the door, in ripples, like miniature dunes.

'He's dead,' I supposed, remembering his brightness. Kestrel was so dark, like steel. And infallible.

'I guess so,' said Kestrel.

'Ah, who was he?'

'Search me,' said Kestrel, with a shrug. 'Some nut, who thought he was Moses or something.'

'Not Moses,' Byrne said. 'Lucifer.'

I had forgotten him. A voice from the dead. His eyes were dead too, lightless, mere black holes in a face that meteorites throughout the ages had riddled with craters.

249

'He thought Christ was Lucifer too. Trying to make good and go home.'

'I told you,' Kestrel said. 'A pisswit of the first water.'

And I watched the tiny red sandhills struggling in under the door.

'Ah, go,' I begged them. 'Go, please.'

'There's one thing,' Kestrel said.

'What?'

'You'll hear the bell, when this is over. Come to the church.'

'To the church,' I repeated, sighing. 'Why?'

'I'm the pope here now,' said Kestrel. And grinned. With silver eyes and black lashes.

I couldn't look at him any longer. I laid my head down, among the pages of my testament.

'Come on,' Kestrel said to Byrne. Then a great blast of wind came in, fluttering the papers under me until the door slammed again. And when I looked up the lamps had blown out, and I was alone. In a room of pale stone, ledges heaped with dust, a safe filled with gold in one corner. It was nearly dark. Only a thick red gloom came in through the windows, like the glow of a dying fire.

I went down the road, battling the wind. Everything was flowing; insubstantial. The obelisk and the hotel would appear through the dust and then, in an instant, melt away.

I opened the door of the store. It tried to break from me. I leaned on it to close it.

Tom was asleep at the counter, his head resting on his forearms. There was dust in his thinning hair. So peaceful he looked. I felt calmed.

The wind hissed through the rafters, and among the bridles and halters and saddles rotting and rusting there. Occasional sounds of pots and dishes came from the kitchen.

'Tom,' I said. He did not stir.

I reached over and touched his arm, gently.

Dust lay on his arm. There was nothing I could say.

In the kitchen Mary was kneading dough. I took her floury hands. 'Mary,' I said. 'Oh Mary. Tom is dead.'

And she cried as a child does, looking straight at you, and crumpling.

I walked out, into the thick red wind.

It was like swimming under water, in a flooding river. Dust sifted into my lungs; I was drowning.

And the bell, up on the hill, kept tolling. Purposeless; moved by the wind.

There was no town, no hill, no landscape. There was nothing. Only myself, swimming through the red flood, that had covered the world and spared me only, of all those who had been there.

Dust lay over the chimneys of Lacey's Find; over the lone billiard table in the desert. It silted up the stock route well at Dave Speed's camp. It heaped in the sockets of the diviner's eyes.

Wild beasts were loose on the world. Terrors would come. But wonders, too, as in the past. Terrors and wonders, as always.

I have seen rain in Tourmaline. Can you believe that? How can you? You have not seen that green, that green like burning, that covers all the stones on the red earth, and glows, gently, upward, till the grey-green leaves of the myall are drab no longer, but green as the grass, washed in reflected light. And the fragrance then; the turpentine weed, the balm. Birds in the air; sheep in the far green distance. And pools, lakes, oceans of blowing flowers.

I have seen rain in Tourmaline. I am not young.

And Kestrel's hair is growing thinner.

There is no sin but cruelty. Only one. And that original sin, that began when a man first cried to another, in his matted hair: Take charge of my life, I am close to breaking.

The bell tolled. The thick wind whirled. Caught in the current, drowning, I ceased to struggle, and let it bear me up the road. There was no town, no landscape. What could this be if not the end of the world?

Then the wind dropped for half a minute. And I saw my tower, the boundary of Tourmaline, waiting.

Beware of my testament!
(Ah, my New Holland; my gold, my darling.)
I say we have a bitter heritage.
That is not to run it down.

Text Classics

The House that Was Eureka
Nadia Wheatley
Introduced by Toni Jordan

Happy Valley
Patrick White
Introduced by Peter Craven

I for Isobel
Amy Witting
Introduced by Charlotte Wood

Isobel on the Way to the Corner Shop
Amy Witting
Introduced by Maria Takolander

I Own the Racecourse!
Patricia Wrightson
Introduced by Kate Constable

textclassics.com.au